LITTLE MOUSE

Gets Ready

JEFF SMITH

Little Mouse
Gets Ready

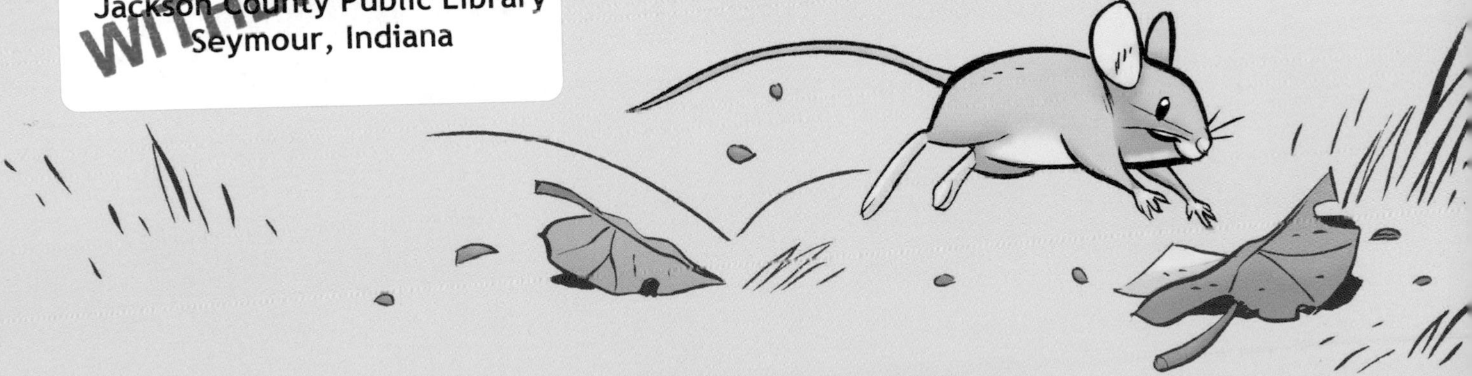

A TOON BOOK BY

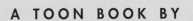

JEFF SMITH

TOON BOOKS IS AN IMPRINT OF CANDLEWICK PRESS

ABDO Spotlight

For Kathleen Glosan

Editorial Director: FRANÇOISE MOULY
Book Design: JONATHAN BENNETT & FRANÇOISE MOULY
Colors: STEVE HAMAKER
JEFF SMITH'S artwork was drawn in black ink on paper and digitally colored.

ABDOPUBLISHING.COM

Reinforced library bound edition published in 2015 by Spotlight, a division of ABDO, PO Box 398166, Minneapolis, Minnesota 55439. Spotlight produces high-quality reinforced library bound editions for schools and libraries. Published by agreement with Candlewick Press.

Printed in the United States of America, North Mankato, Minnesota.
112014
012015

THIS BOOK CONTAINS
RECYCLED MATERIALS

LIBRARY OF CONGRESS CATALOGING-IN-PUBLICATION DATA

This book was previously cataloged with the following information:

Smith, Jeff, 1960 Feb. 27-
 Little Mouse gets ready / by Jeff Smith.
 p. cm.   "A Toon Book."
 Summary: Little Mouse gets dressed to go to the barn with his mother, brothers, and sisters.
 ISBN 978-1-935179-01-6
 1. Graphic novels. [1. Graphic novels. 2. Mice—Fiction. 3. Clothing and dress—Fiction.] I. Title.
 PZ7.7.S64Li 2009   741.5'973--dc22   2008055403

978-1-61479-301-4 (reinforced library bound edition)

Spotlight
A Division of ABDO
abdopublishing.com

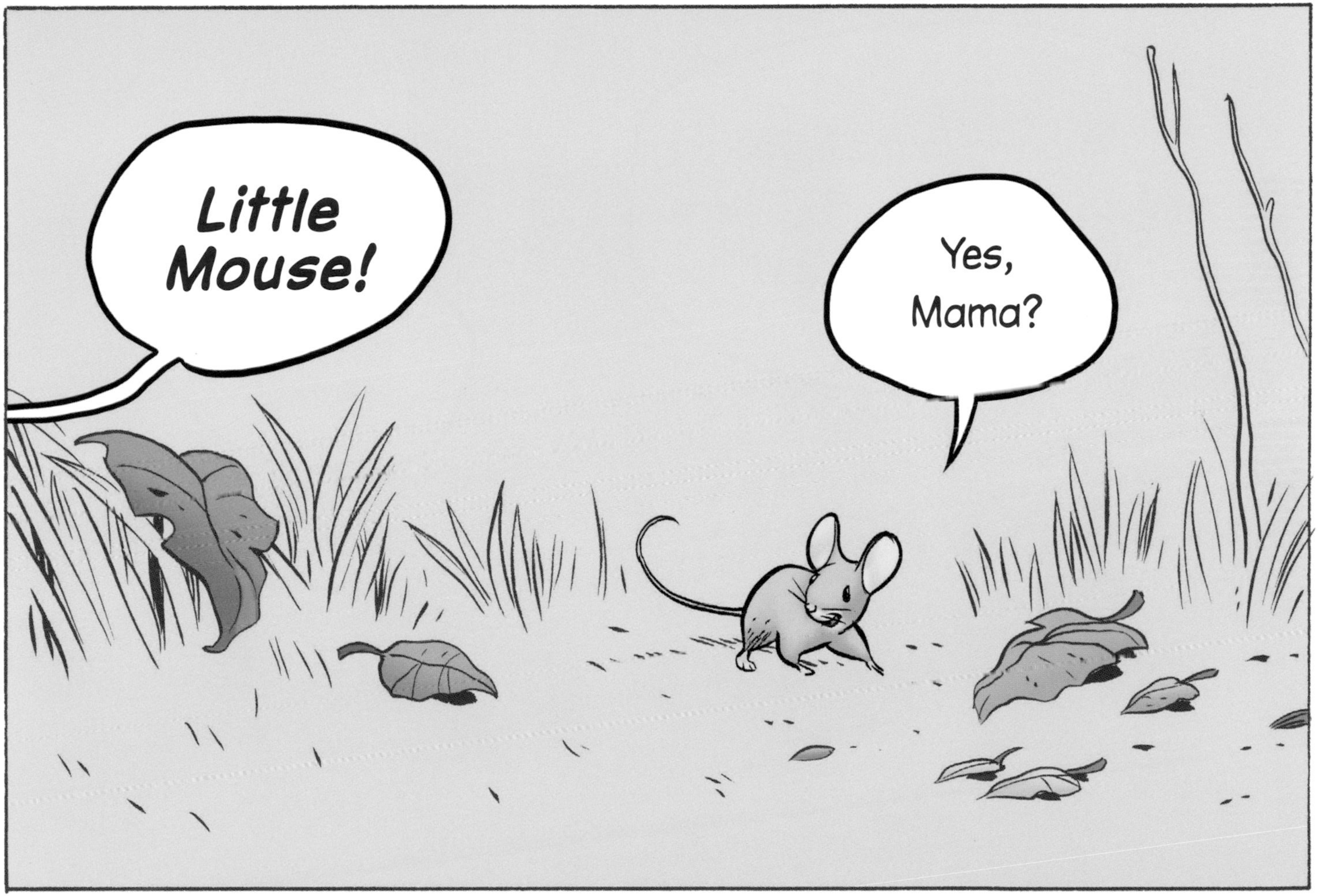
Little Mouse!
Yes, Mama?

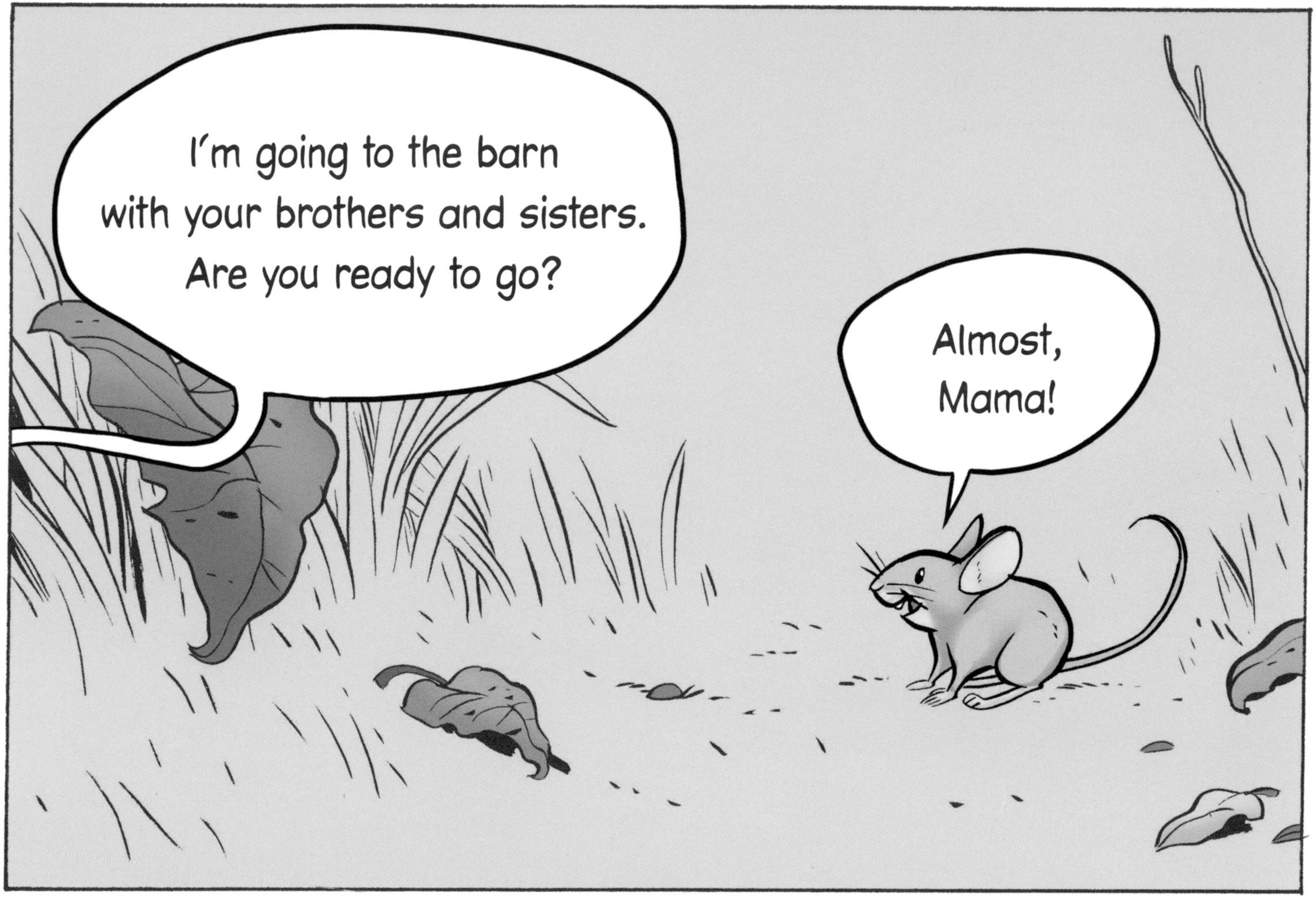
I'm going to the barn with your brothers and sisters. Are you ready to go?
Almost, Mama!

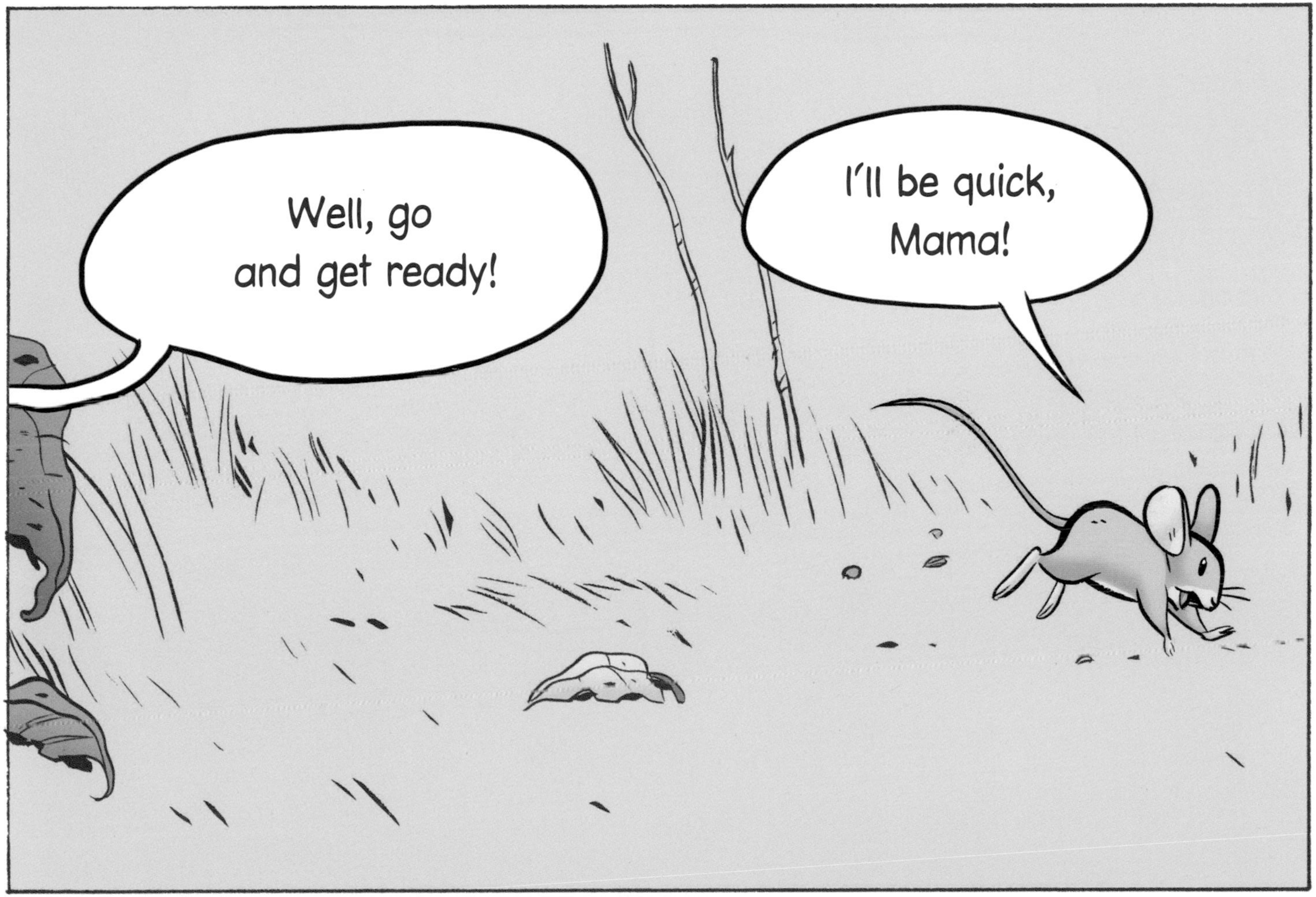
Well, go
and get ready!
I'll be quick,
Mama!

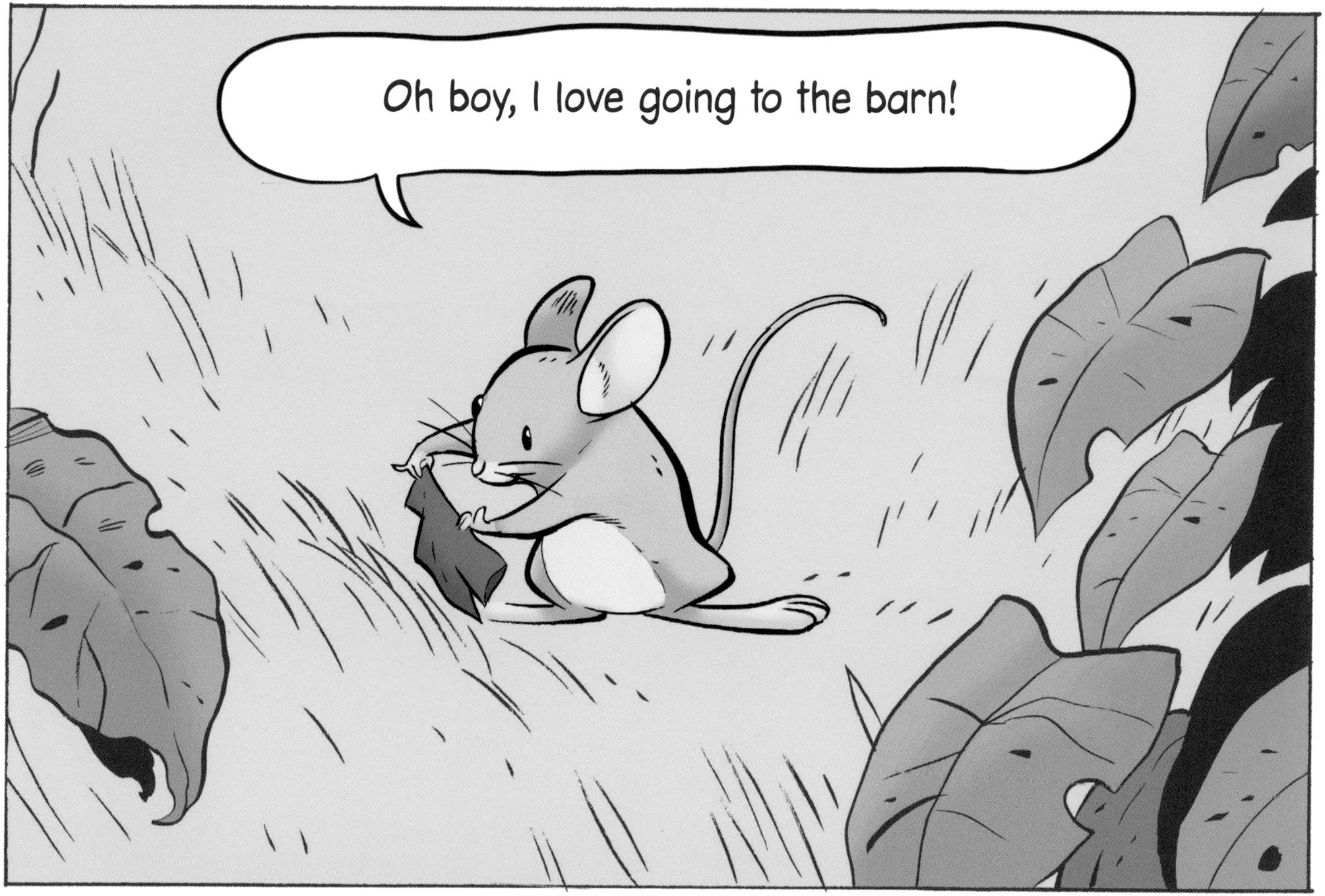
Oh boy, I love going to the barn!

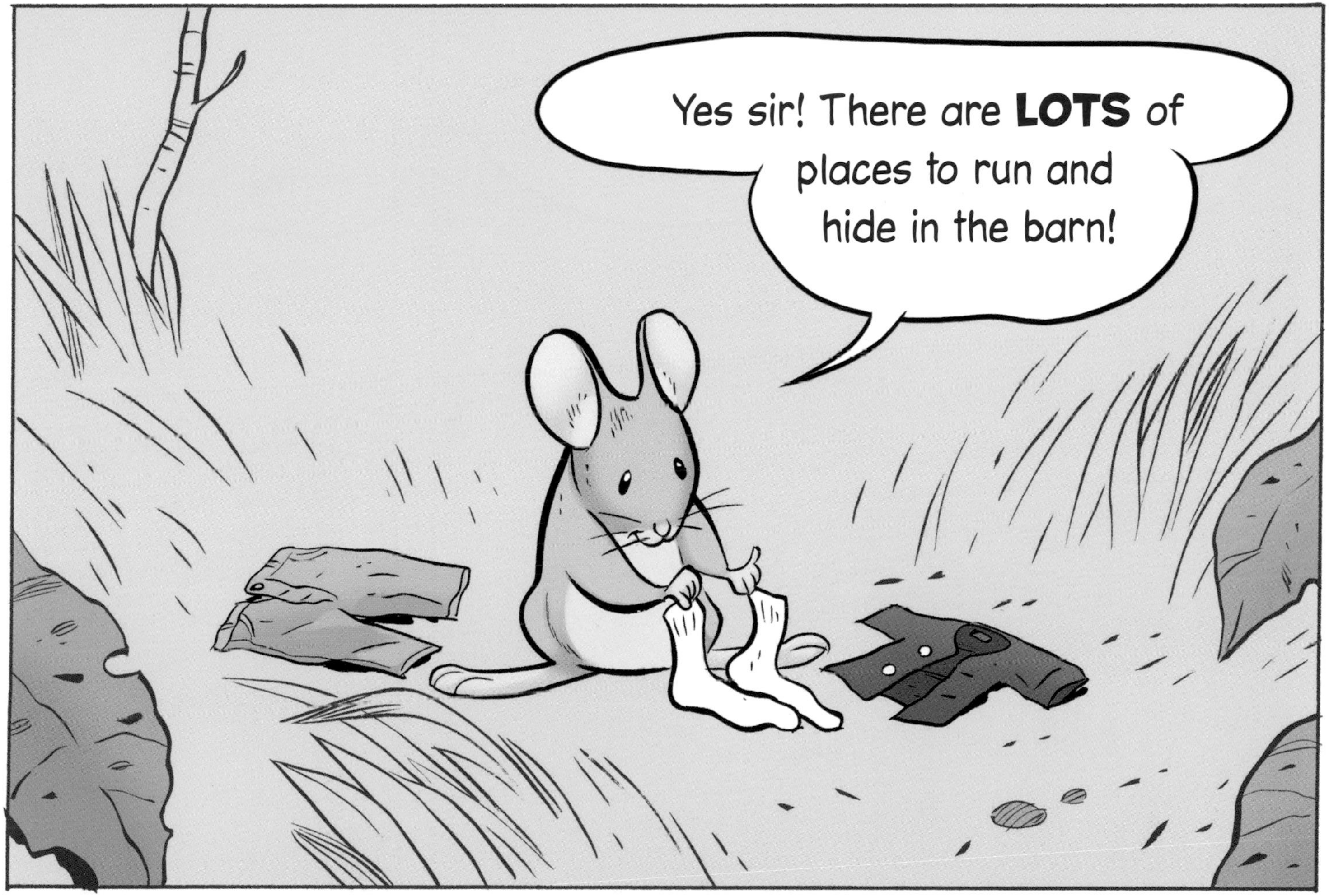
Yes sir! There are **LOTS** of places to run and hide in the barn!

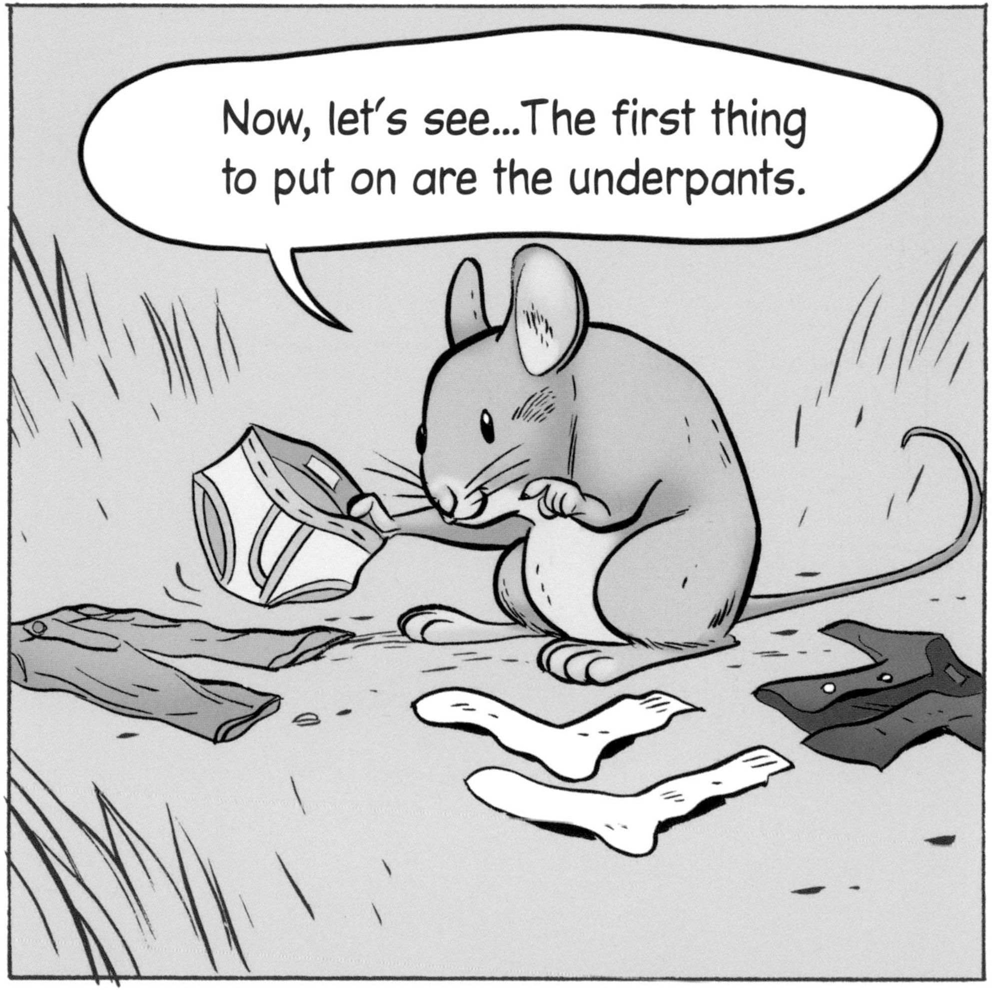
Now, let's see...The first thing to put on are the underpants.

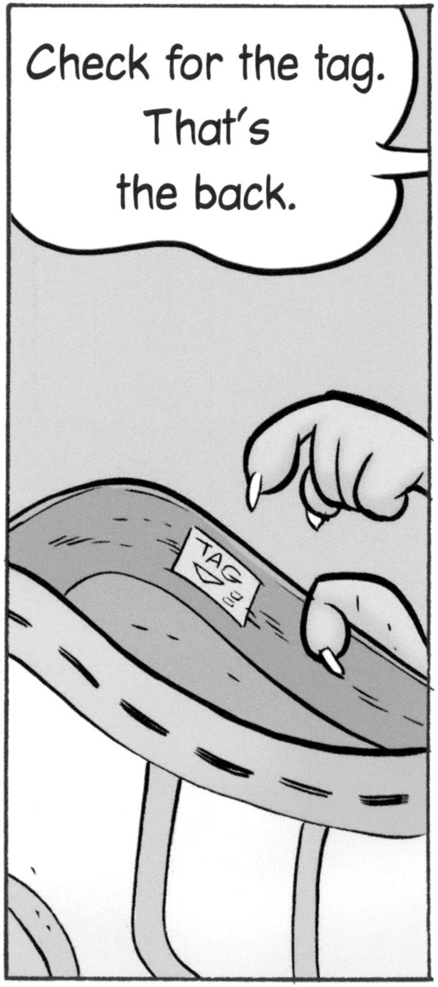
Check for the tag. That's the back.
TAG

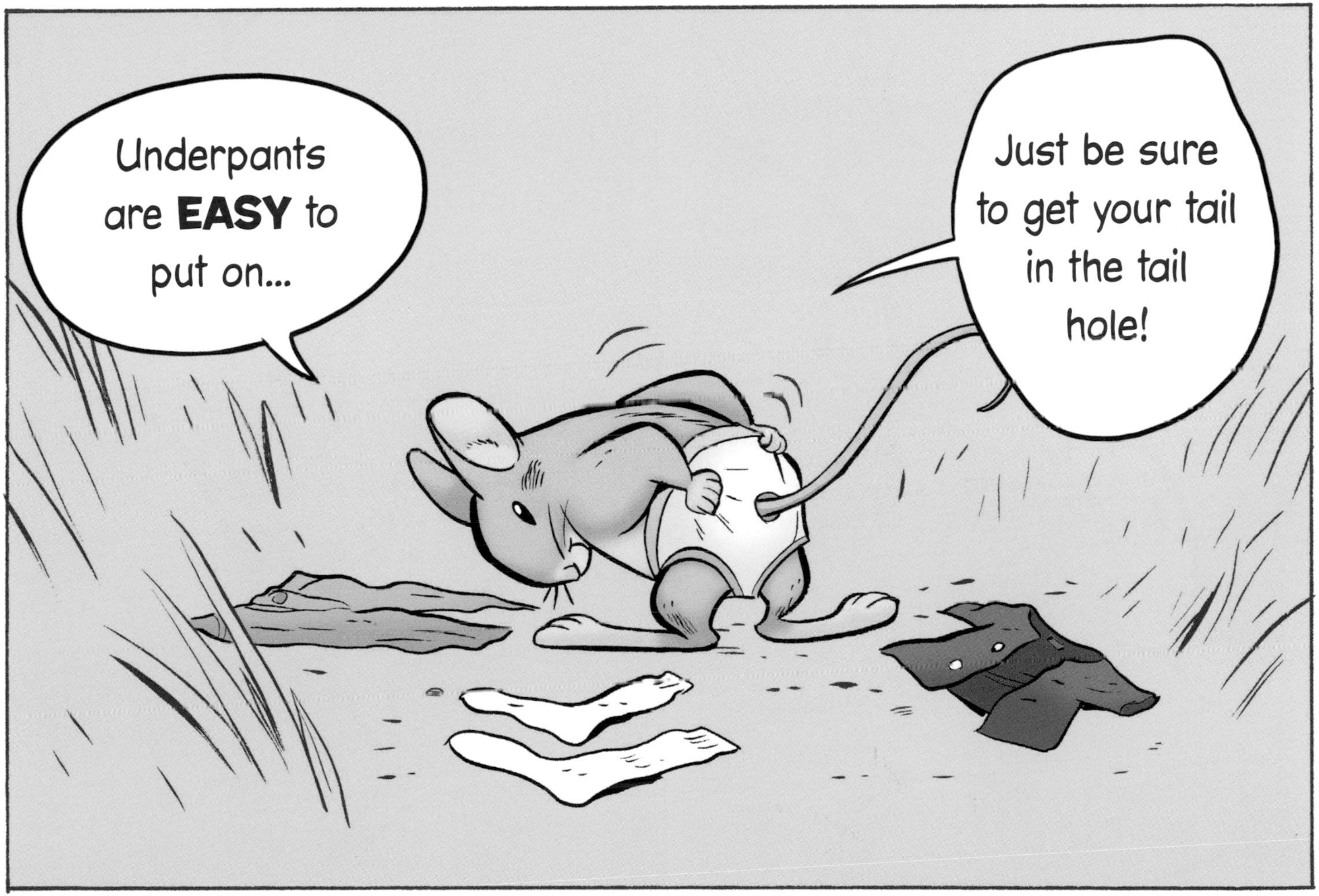
Underpants are **EASY** to put on...
Just be sure to get your tail in the tail hole!

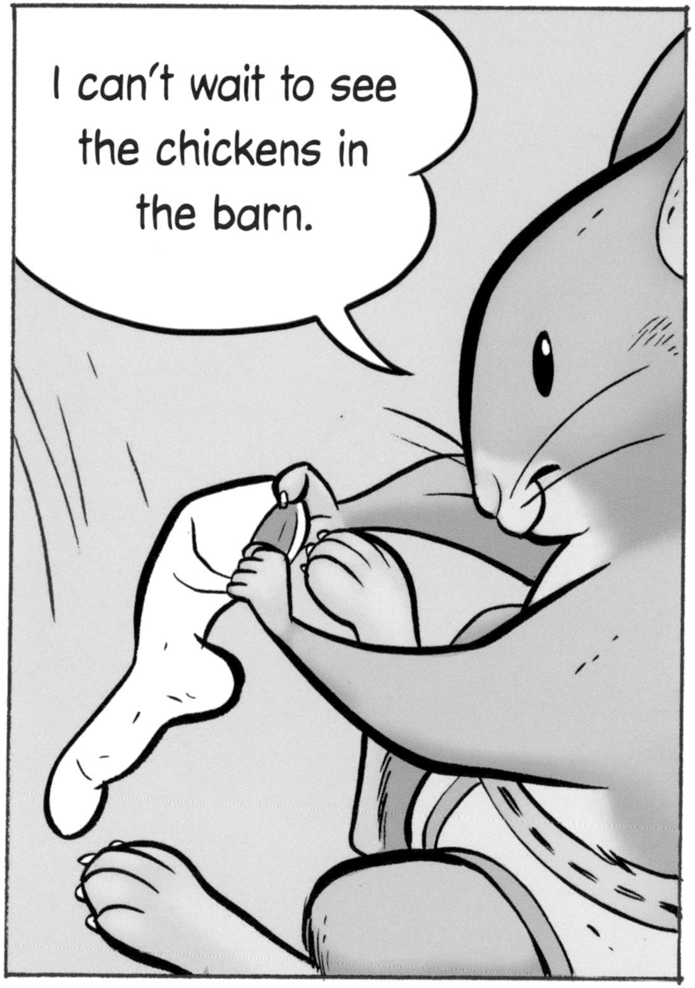
I can't wait to see the chickens in the barn.

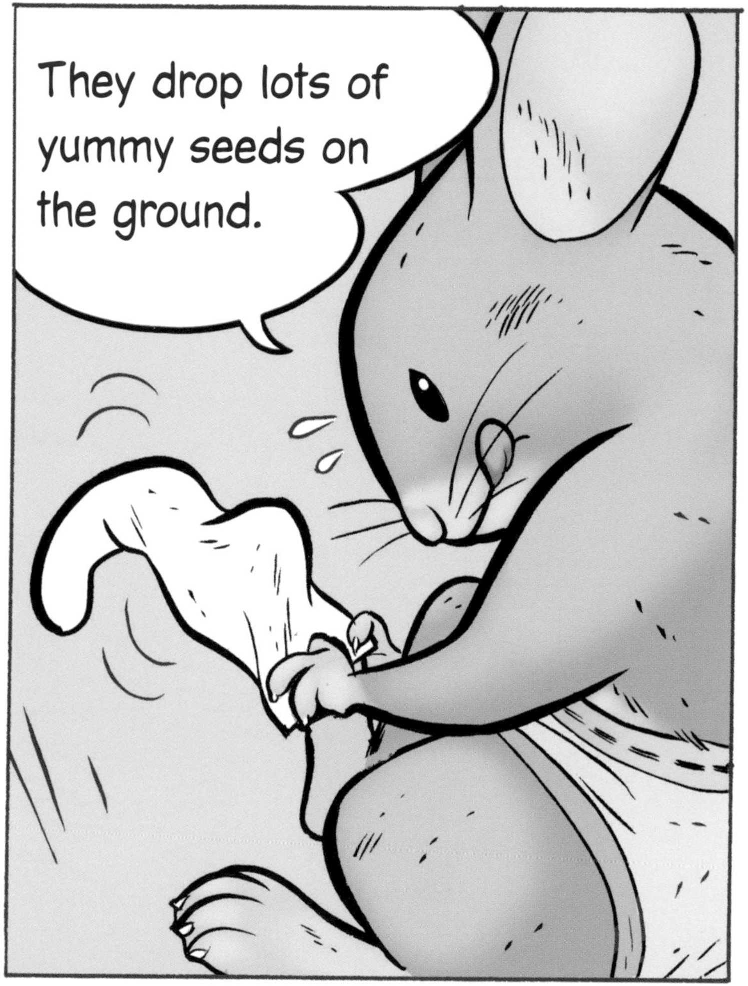
They drop lots of yummy seeds on the ground.

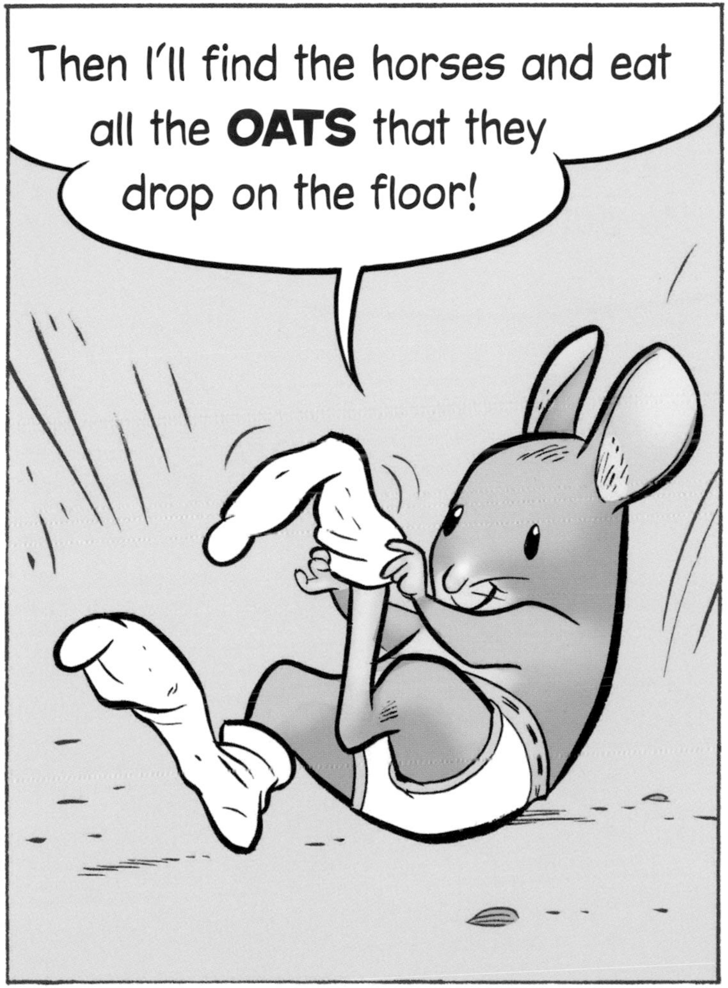
Then I'll find the horses and eat all the **OATS** that they drop on the floor!

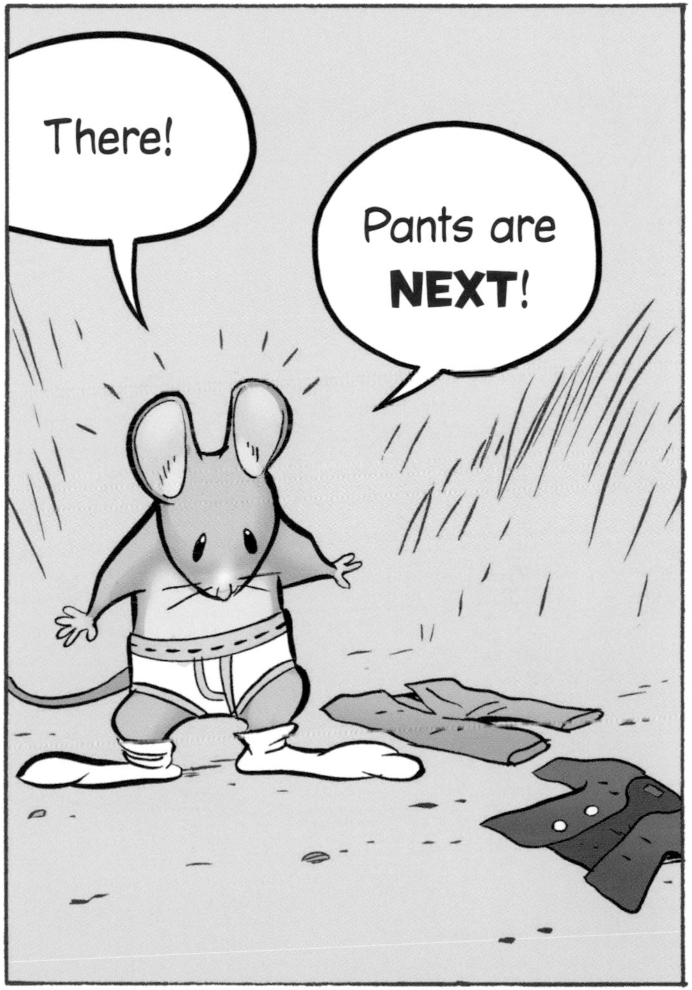
There!
Pants are **NEXT**!

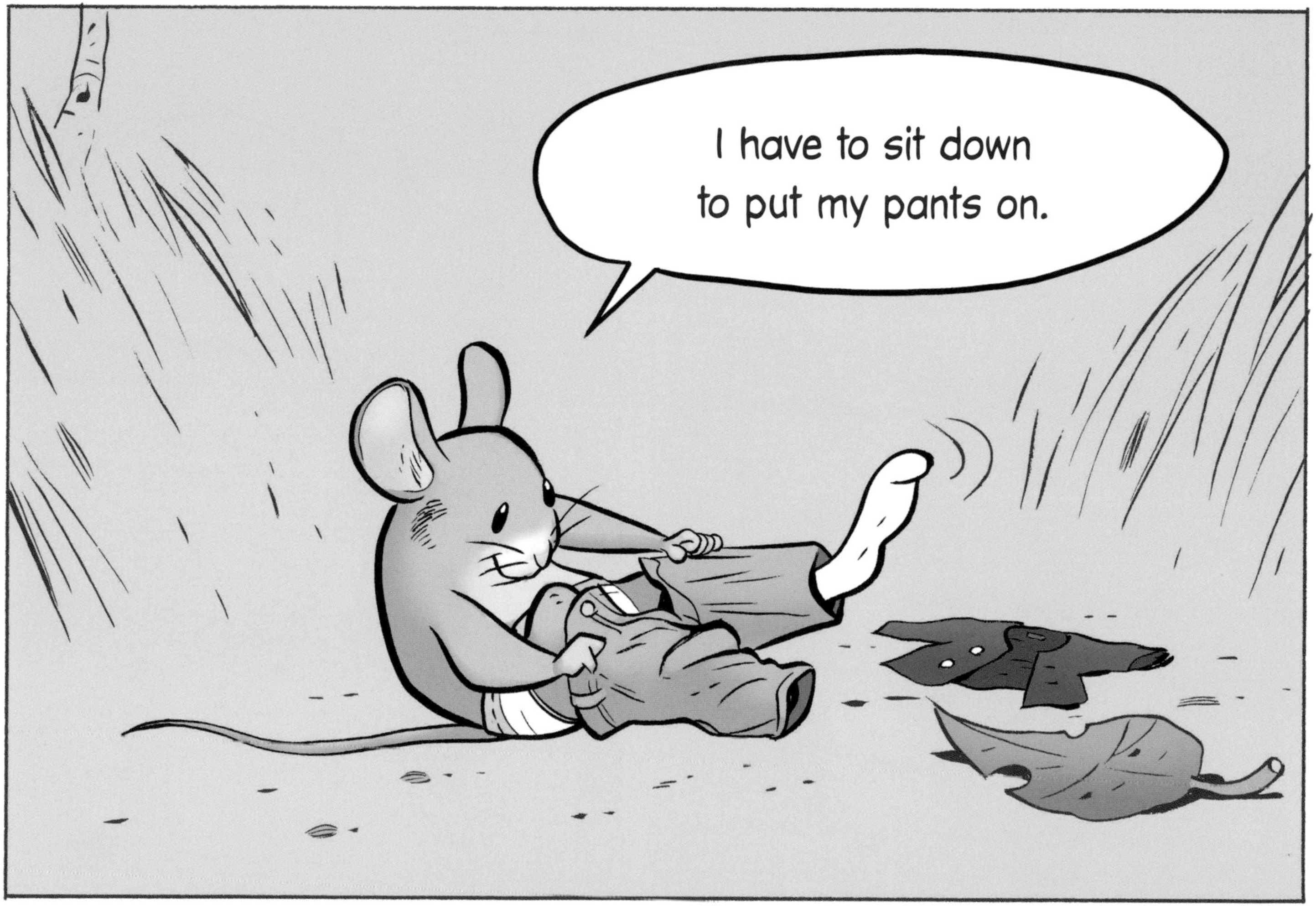
I have to sit down to put my pants on.

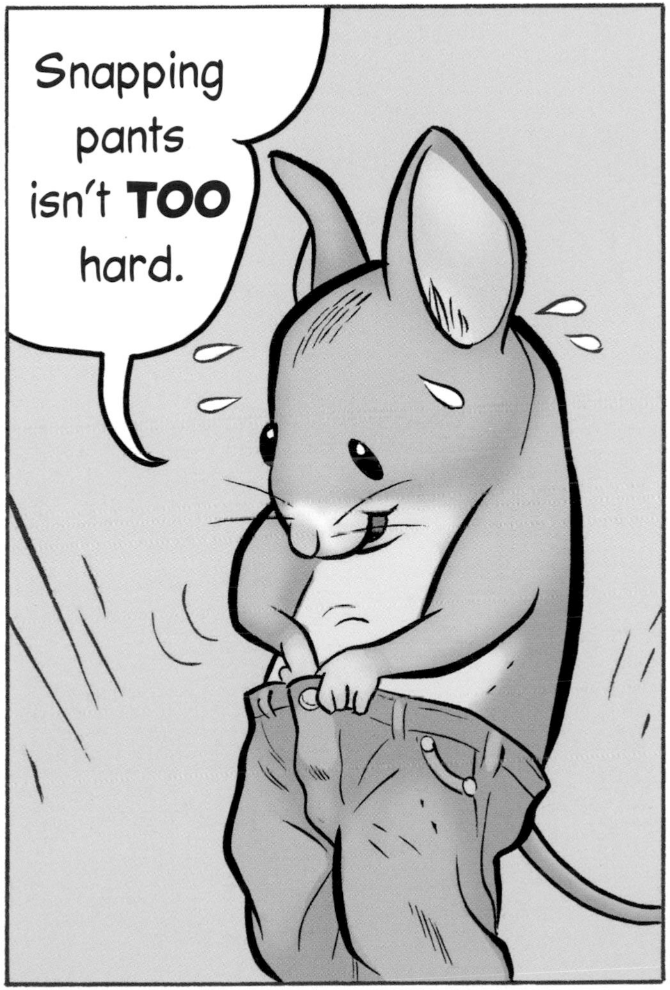
Snapping pants isn't **TOO** hard.

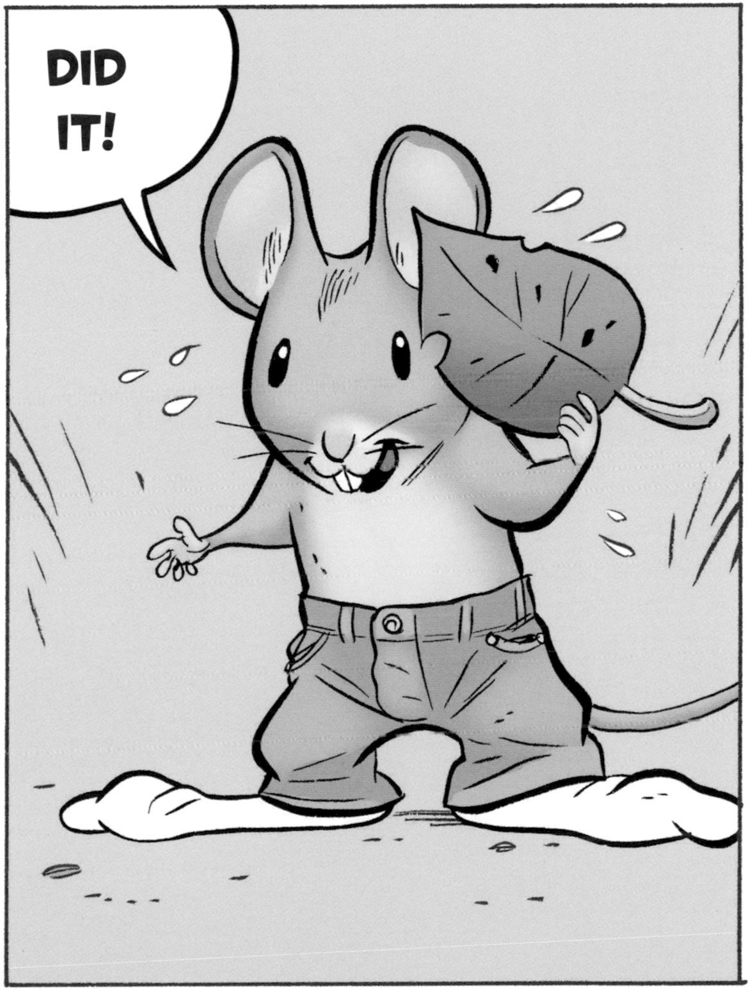
DID IT!

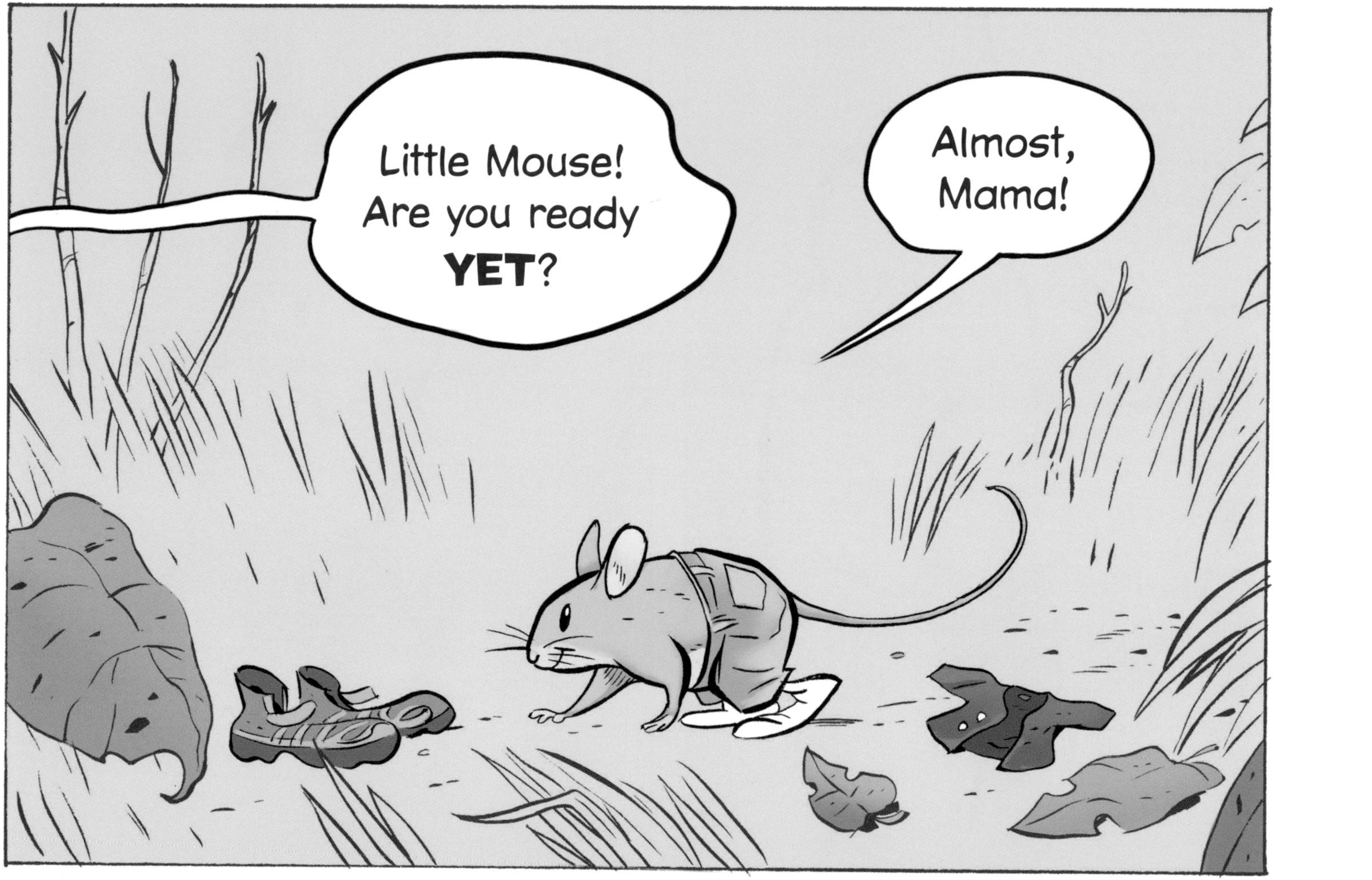
Little Mouse! Are you ready **YET**?
Almost, Mama!

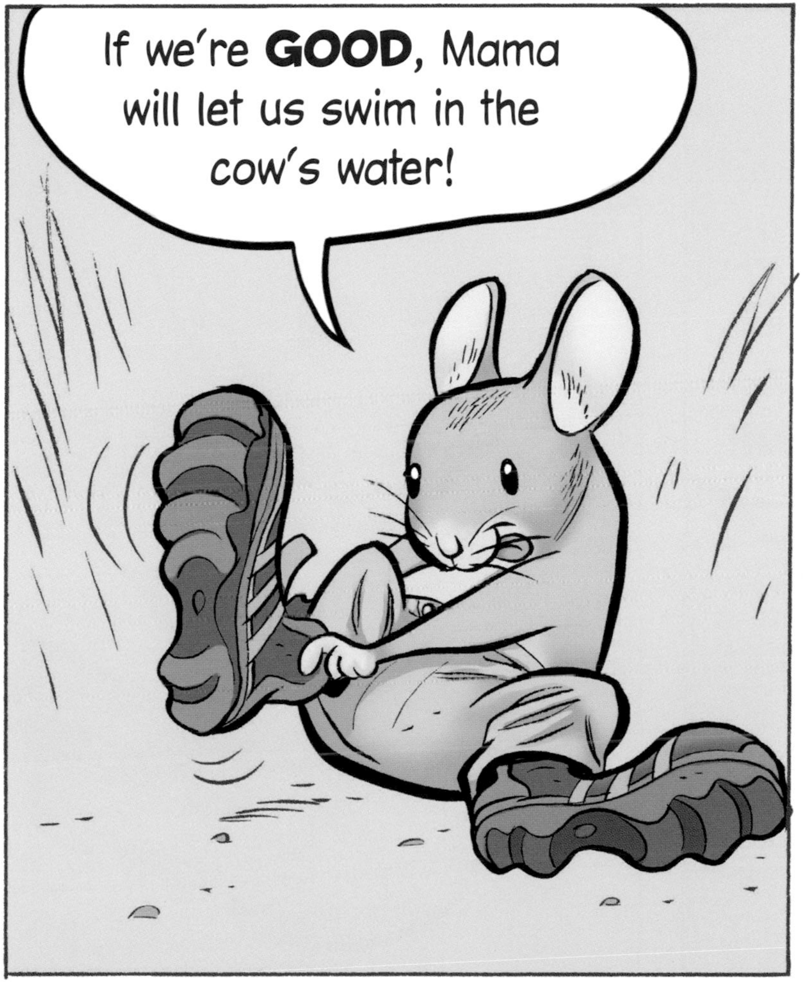
If we're **GOOD**, Mama will let us swim in the cow's water!

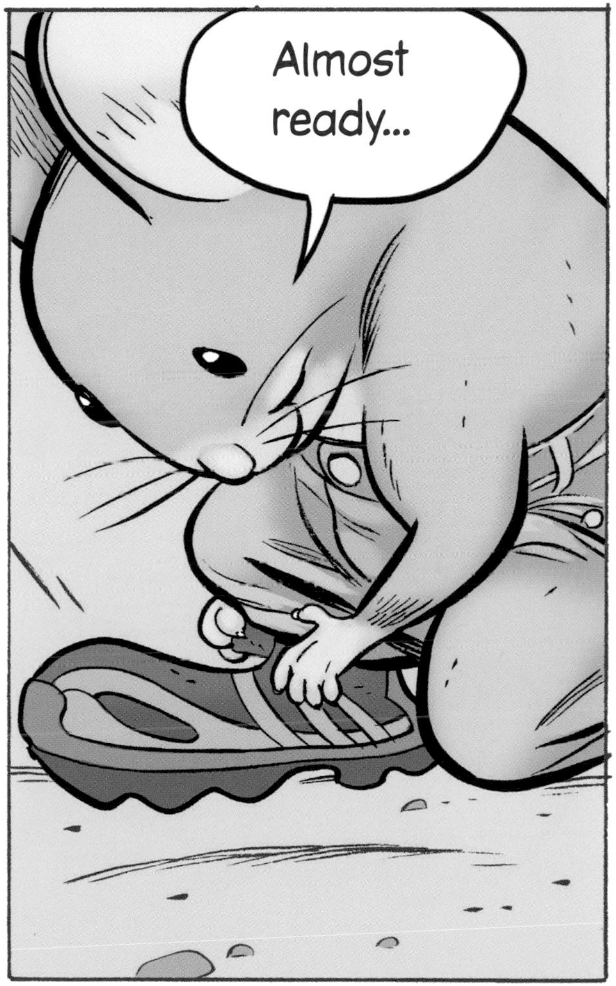
Almost ready...

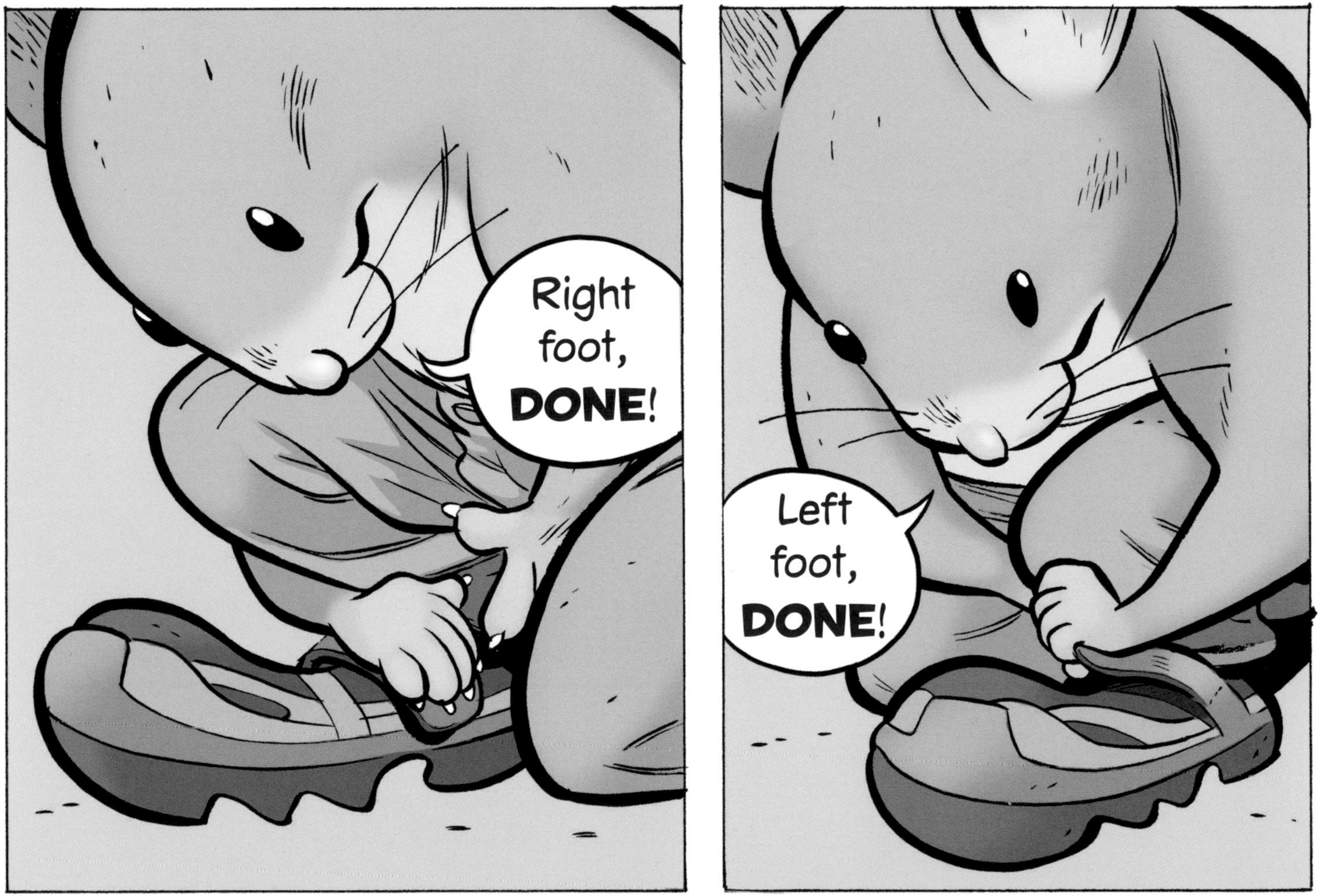
Right foot, **DONE**!
Left foot, **DONE**!

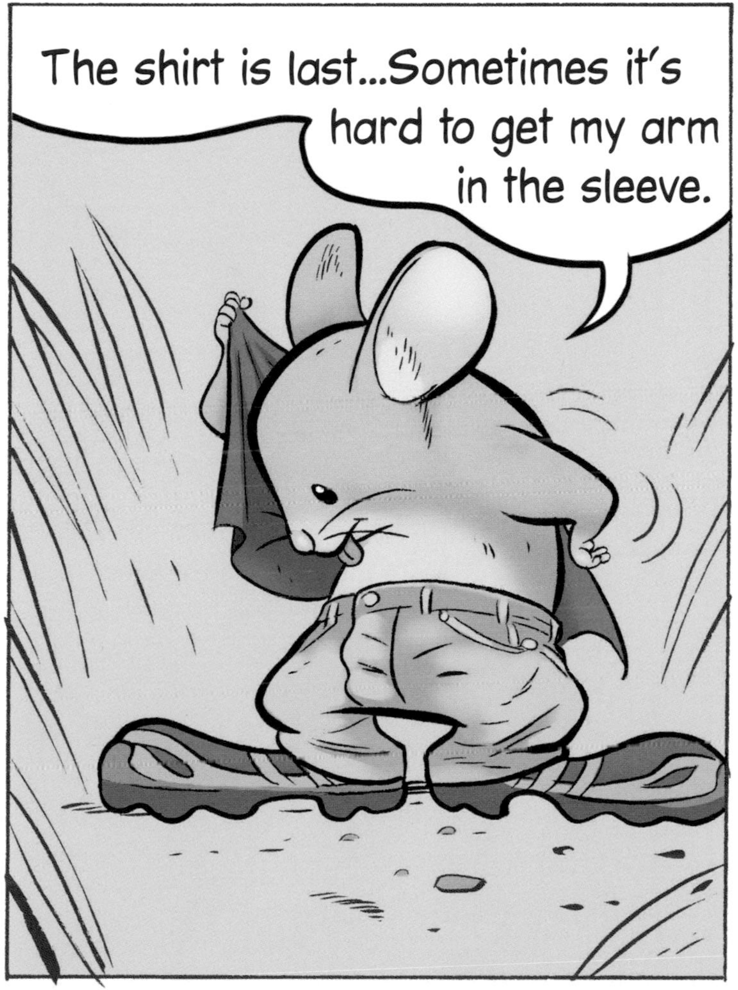
The shirt is last...Sometimes it's hard to get my arm in the sleeve.

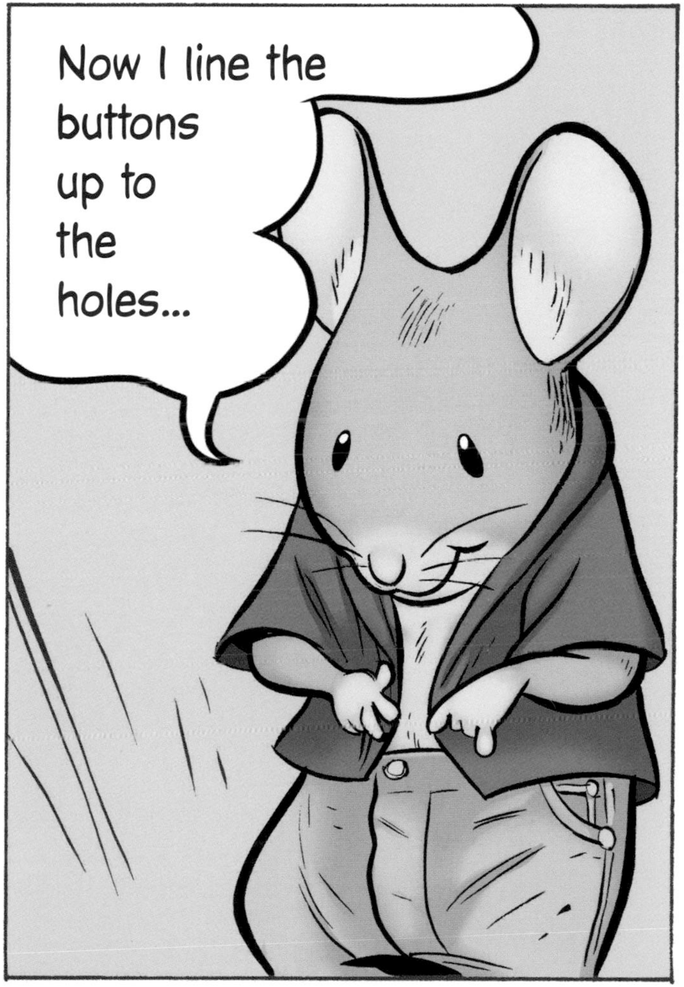
Now I line the buttons up to the holes...

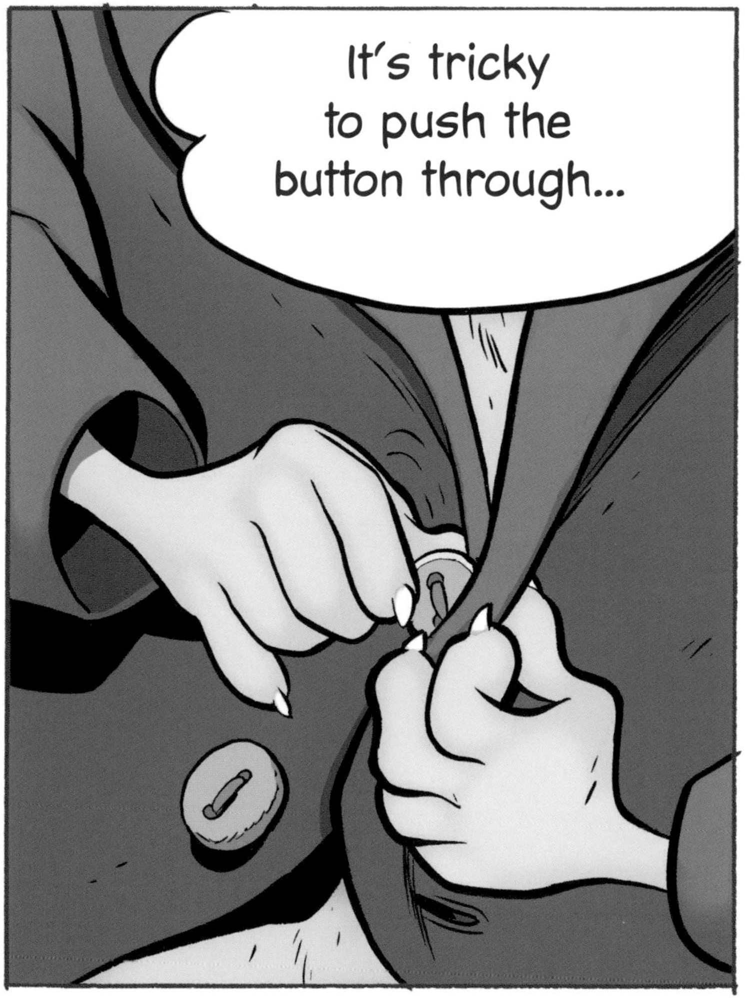
It's tricky to push the button through...

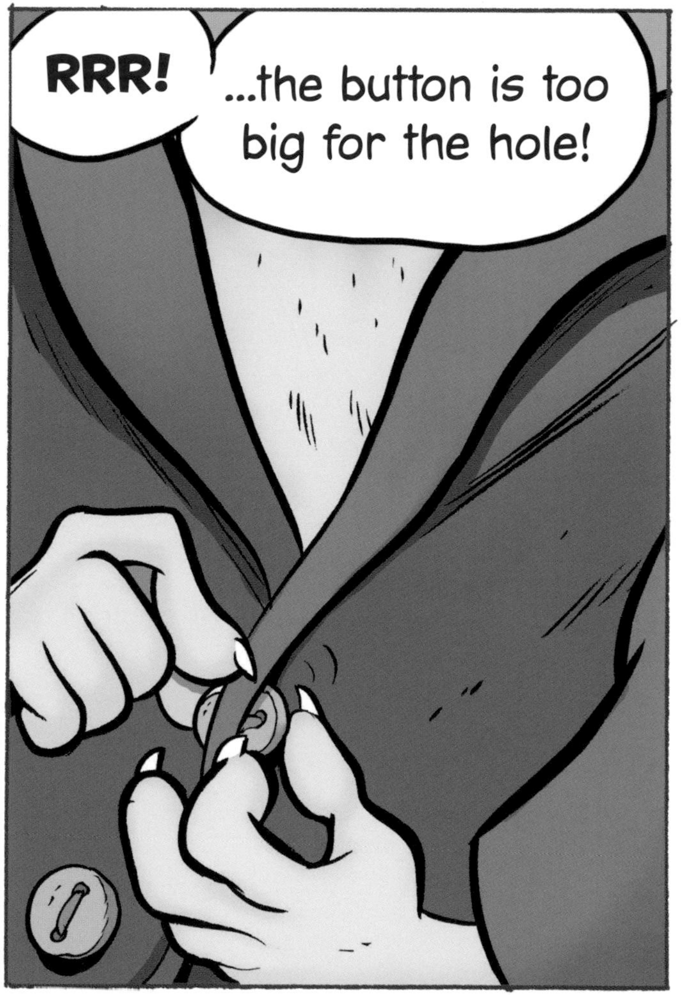
RRR!
...the button is too big for the hole!

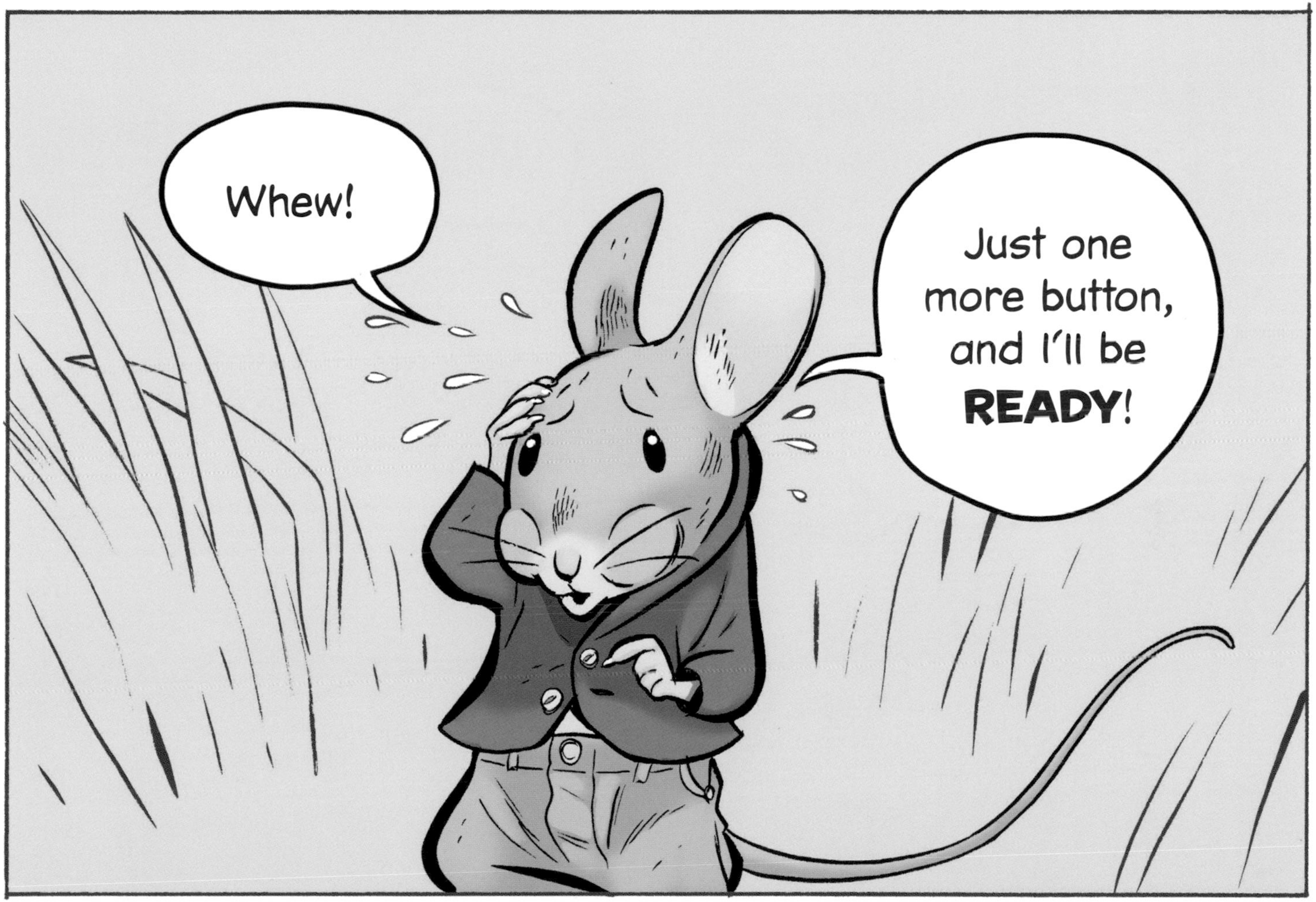
Whew!
Just one more button, and I'll be **READY**!

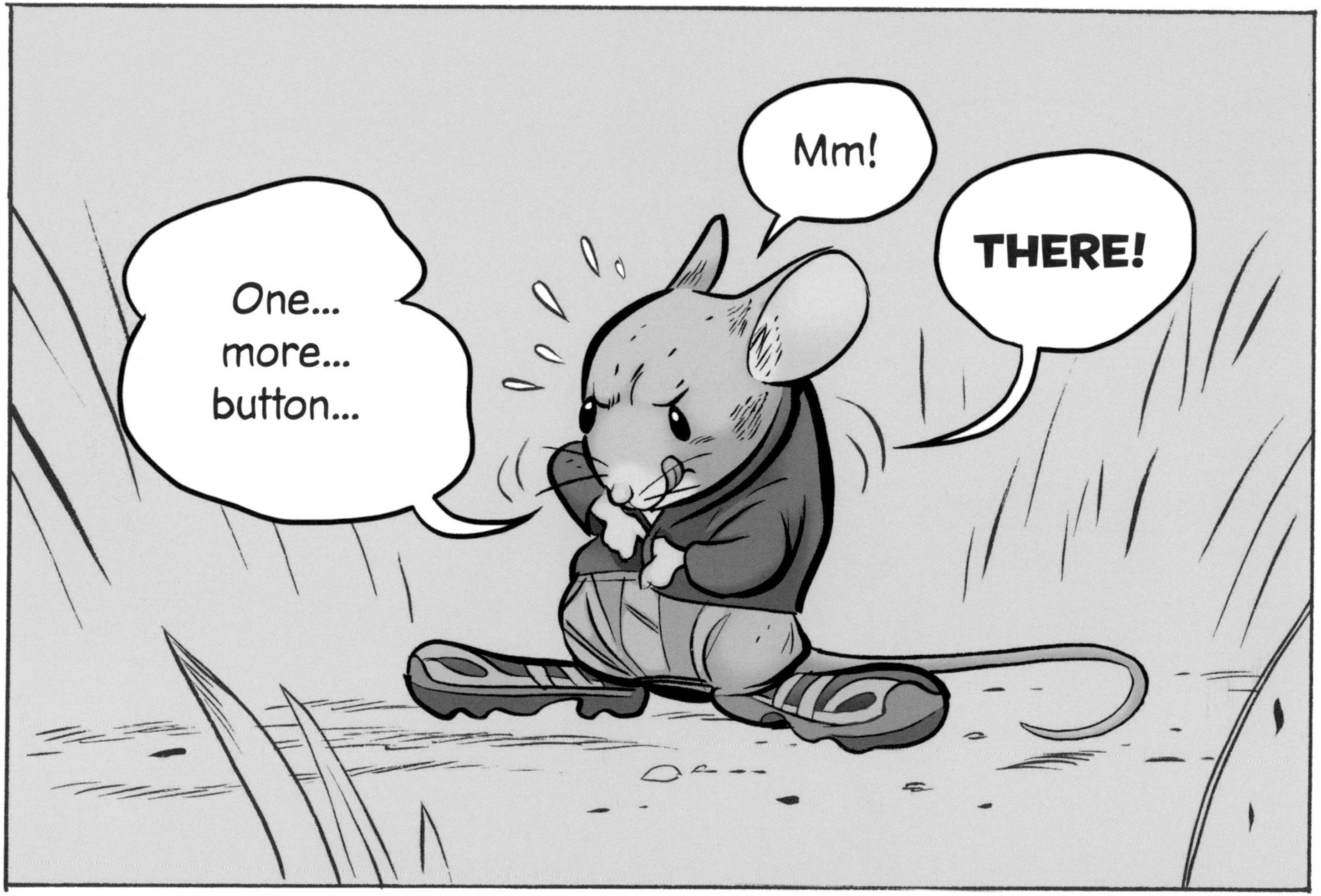
One... more... button...
Mm!
THERE!

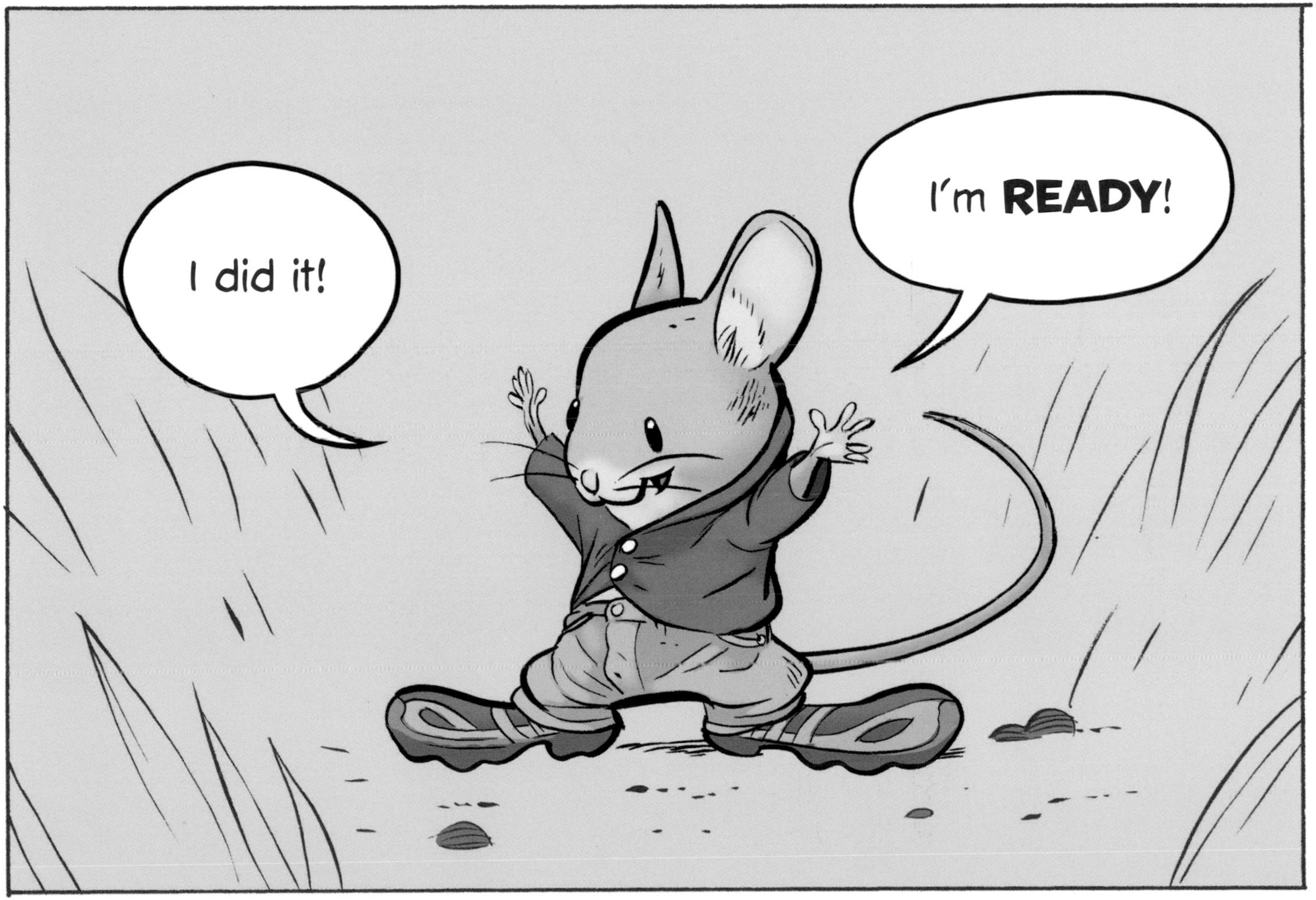
I did it!
I'm **READY**!

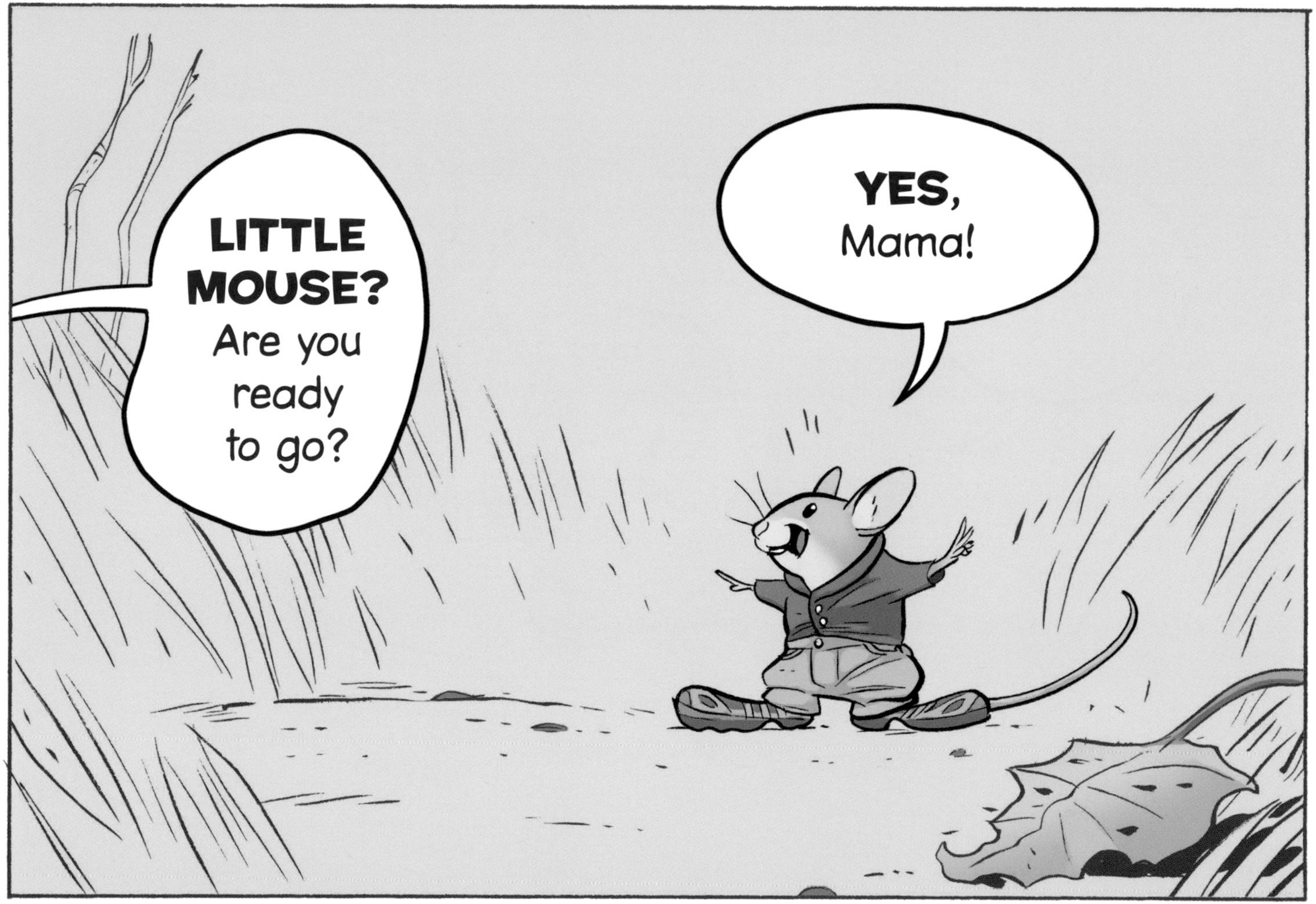
LITTLE MOUSE? Are you ready to go?
YES, Mama!

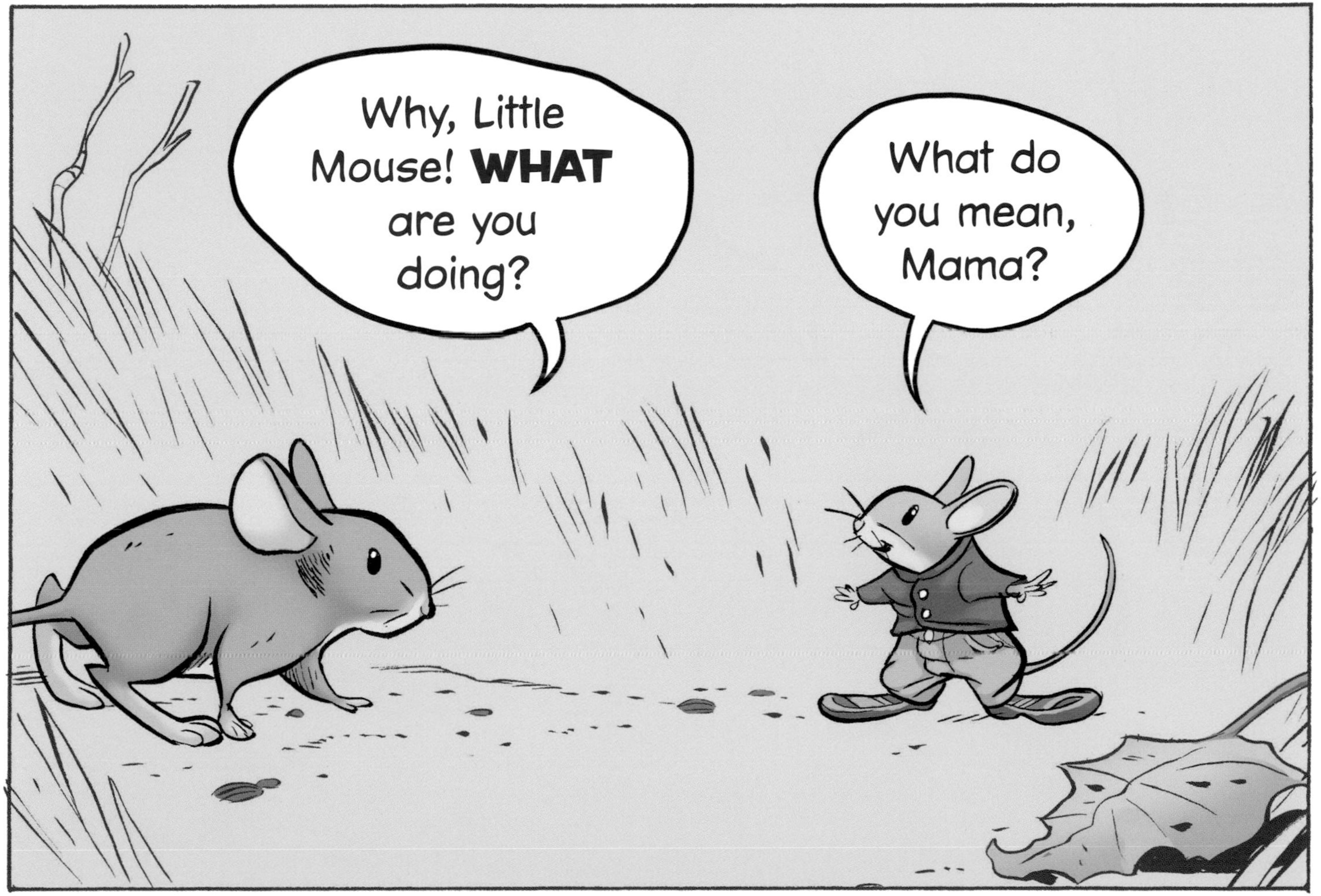
Why, Little Mouse! **WHAT** are you doing?
What do you mean, Mama?

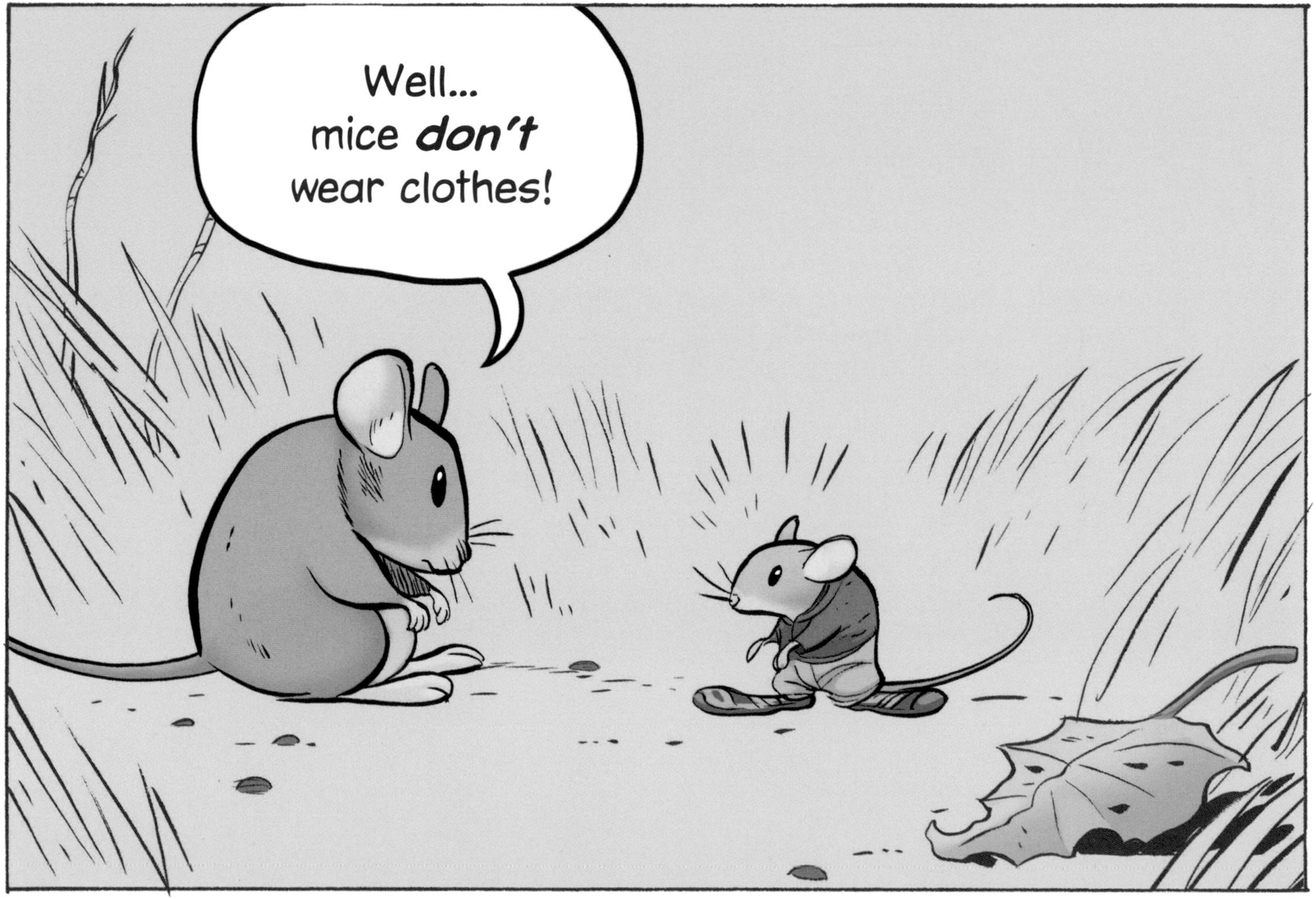
Well... mice ***don't*** wear clothes!

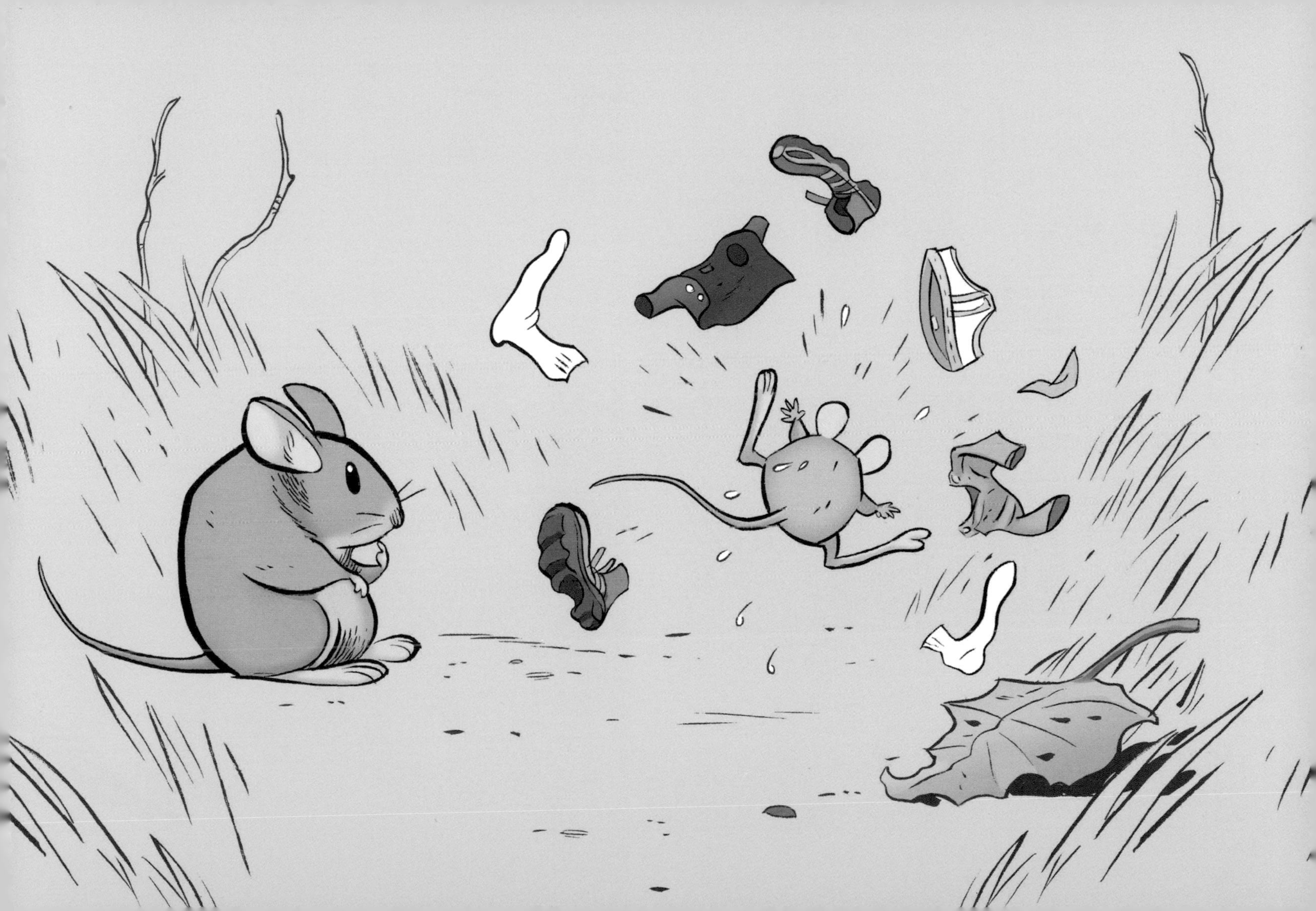

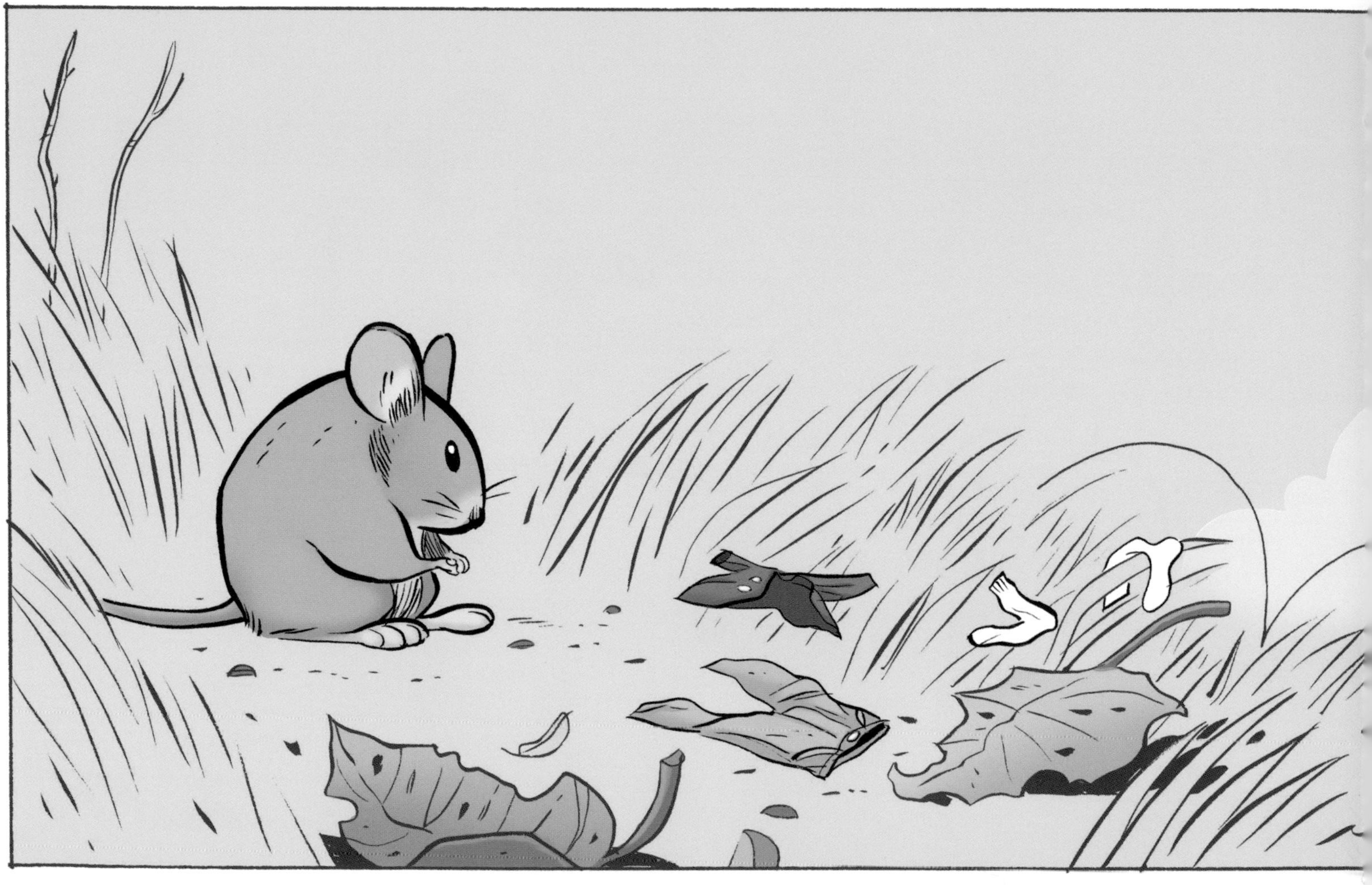

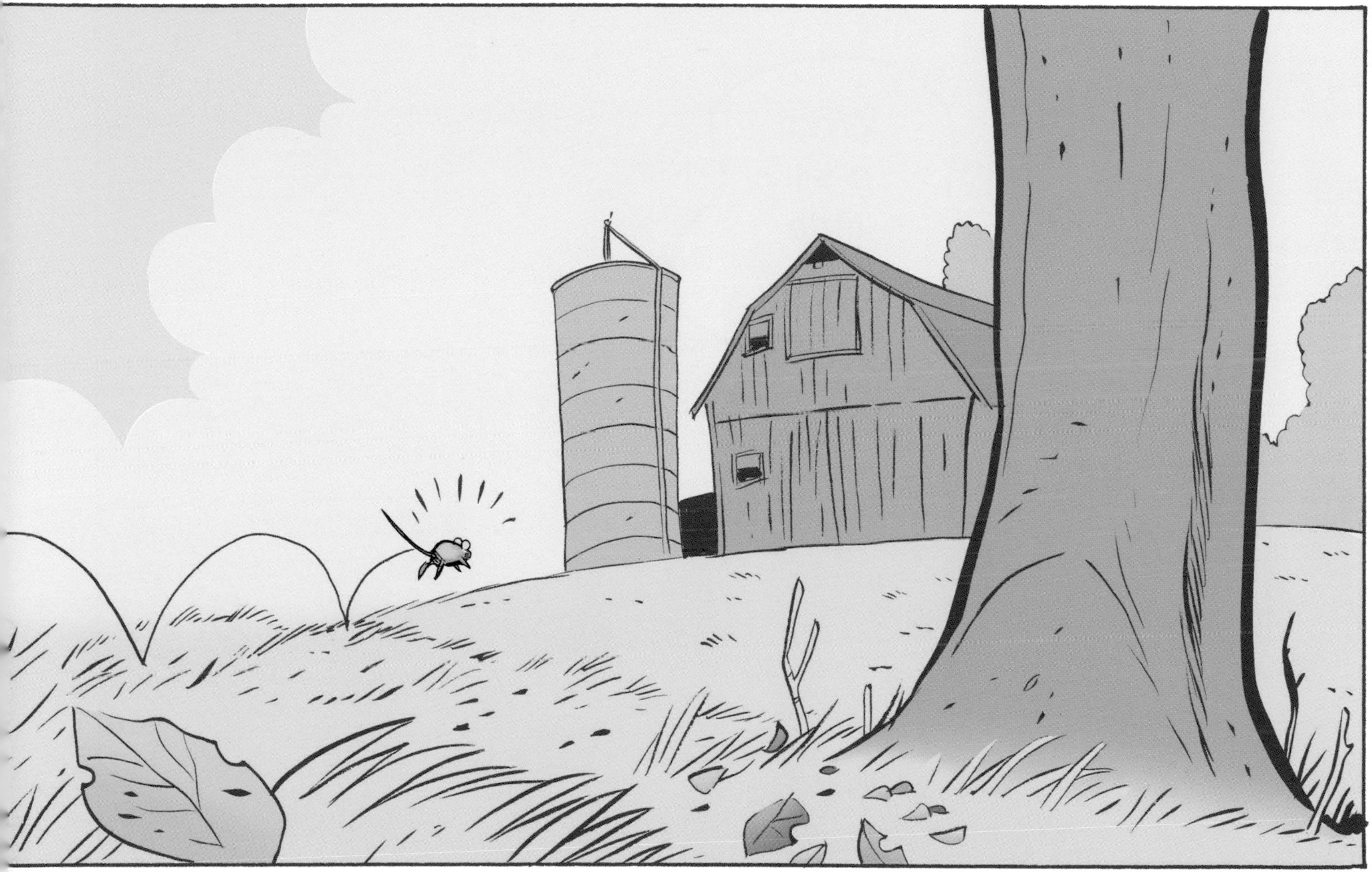

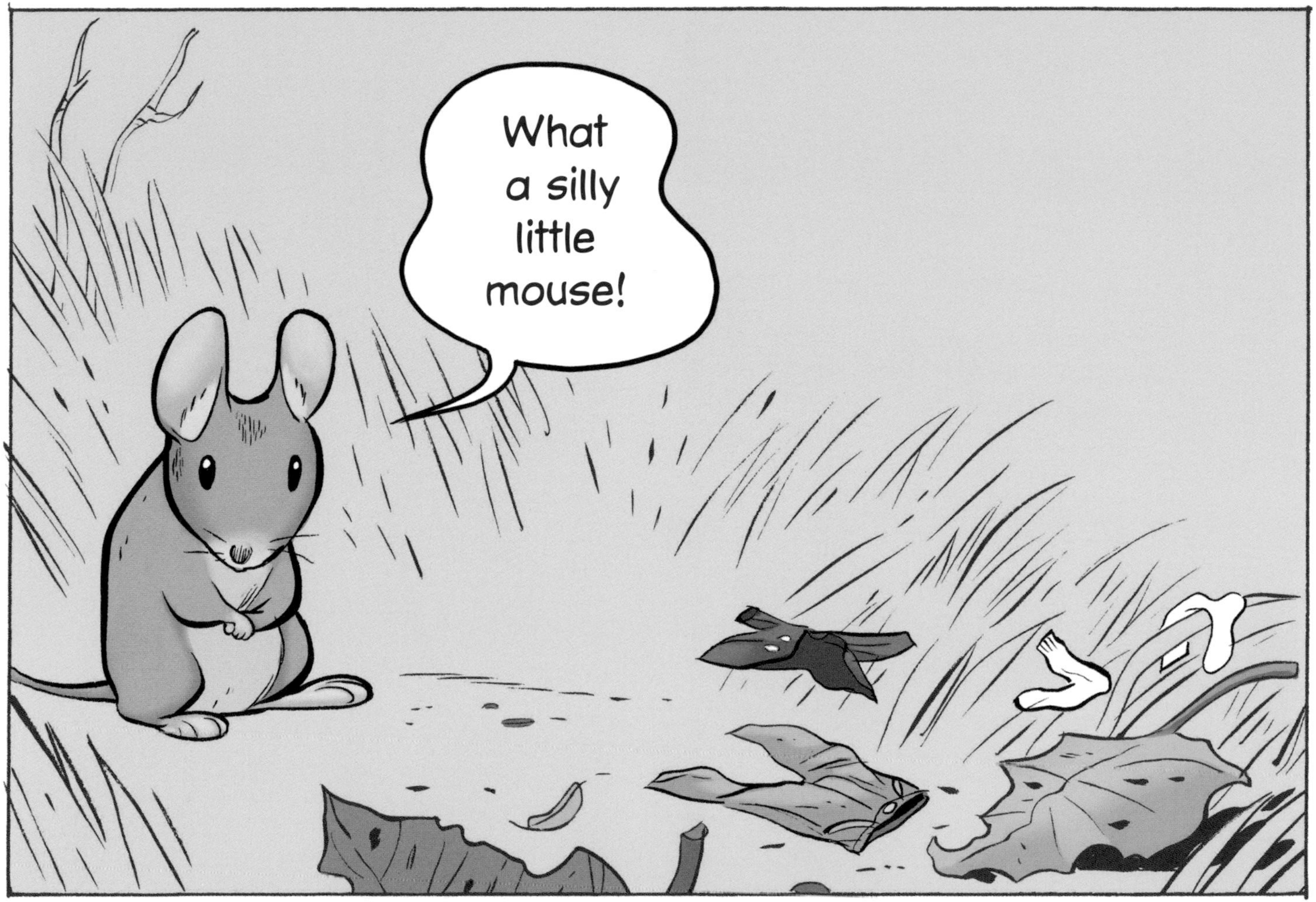
What a silly little mouse!

THE END

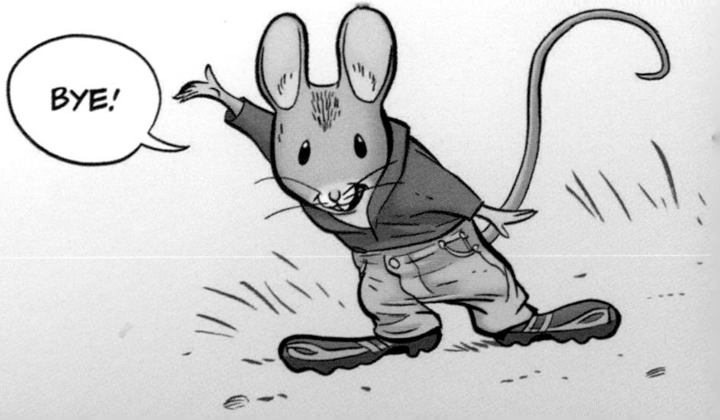
BYE!

ABOUT THE AUTHOR

When **JEFF SMITH** was growing up in a small town in Ohio, he loved cartooning, but he never imagined all the places comics would take him. With the help of his wife, Vijaya, Jeff created, published, and sold his comic book *BONE*. Jeff hadn't created *BONE* specifically for kids, but his fantastic tale of three cousins lost in a strange land appealed to all readers, including children, and it went on to sell millions of copies. *BONE* won multiple Eisner and Harvey Awards, and *TIME* called it one of the ten greatest graphic novels of all time. In 2008, Jeff's work was the subject of a major museum exhibit at the Wexner Center Galleries in Columbus, Ohio. His other books include *Shazam! The Monster Society of Evil* and *RASL*. This is his first book created just for young readers.

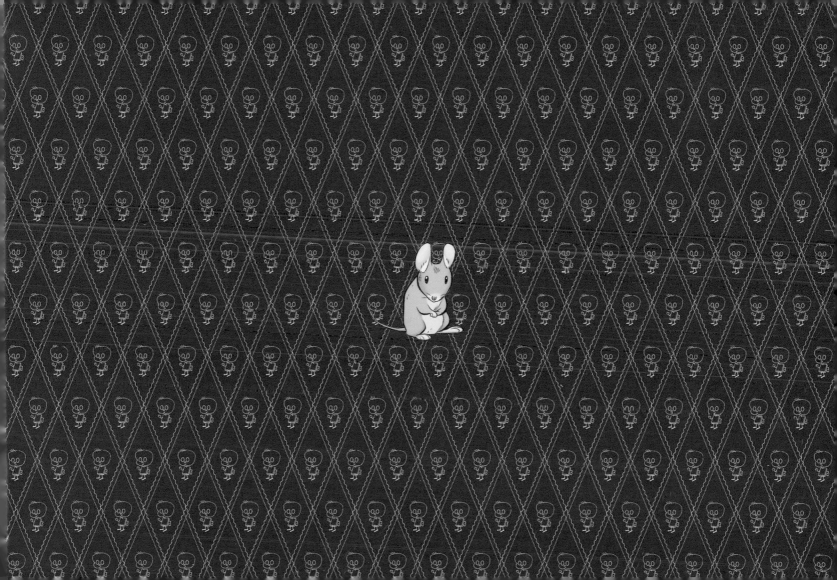

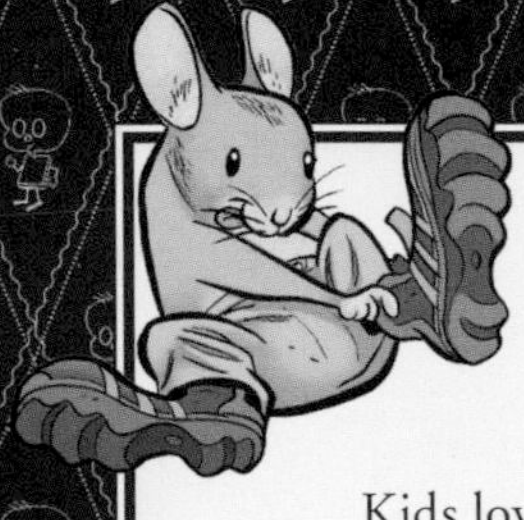

TIPS FOR PARENTS AND TEACHERS:

HOW TO READ COMICS WITH KIDS

Kids love comics! They are naturally drawn to the details in the pictures, which make them want to read the words. Comics beg for repeated readings and let both emerging and reluctant readers enjoy complex stories with a rich vocabulary. But since comics have their own grammar, here are a few tips for reading them with kids:

GUIDE YOUNG READERS: Use your finger to show your place in the text, but keep it at the bottom of the speaking character so it doesn't hide the very important facial expressions.

HAM IT UP! Think of the comic book story as a play and don't hesitate to read with expression and intonation. Assign parts or get kids to supply the sound effects, a great way to reinforce phonics skills.

LET THEM GUESS. Comics provide lots of context for the words, so emerging readers can make informed guesses. Like jigsaw puzzles, comics ask readers to make connections, so check a young audience's understanding by asking "What's this character thinking?" (but don't be surprised if a kid finds some of the comics' subtle details faster than you).

TALK ABOUT THE PICTURES. Point out how the artist paces the story with pauses (silent panels) or speeded-up action (a burst of short panels). Discuss how the size and shape of the panels carry meaning.

ABOVE ALL, ENJOY! There is of course never one right way to read, so go for the shared pleasure. Once children make the story happen in their imagination, they have discovered the thrill of reading, and you won't be able to stop them. At that point, just go get them more books, and more comics.

www.TOON-BOOKS.com

SEE OUR FREE ONLINE CARTOON MAKERS, LESSON PLANS, AND MUCH MORE

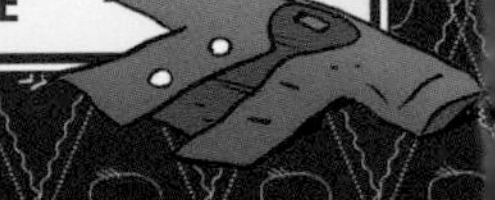

TOON INTO READING

LEVEL 1

FIRST COMICS FOR BRAND-NEW READERS

GRADES K–1 • LEXILE BR–100
GUIDED READING A–G • READING RECOVERY 7–10

- 200–300 easy sight words
- short sentences
- often one character
- single time frame or theme
- 1–2 panels per page

LEVEL 2

EASY-TO-READ COMICS FOR EMERGING READERS

GRADES 1–2 • LEXILE BR–170
GUIDED READING G–J • READING RECOVERY 11–17

- 300–600 words
- short sentences and repetition
- story arc with few characters in a small world
- 1–4 panels per page

LEVEL 3

CHAPTER-BOOK COMICS FOR ADVANCED BEGINNERS

GRADES 2–3 • LEXILE 200–300
GUIDED READING J–N • READING RECOVERY 17–19

- 800–1000+ words
- long sentences
- characters interact with a broad world
- shifts in time and place
- long story divided in chapters

COLLECT THEM ALL!

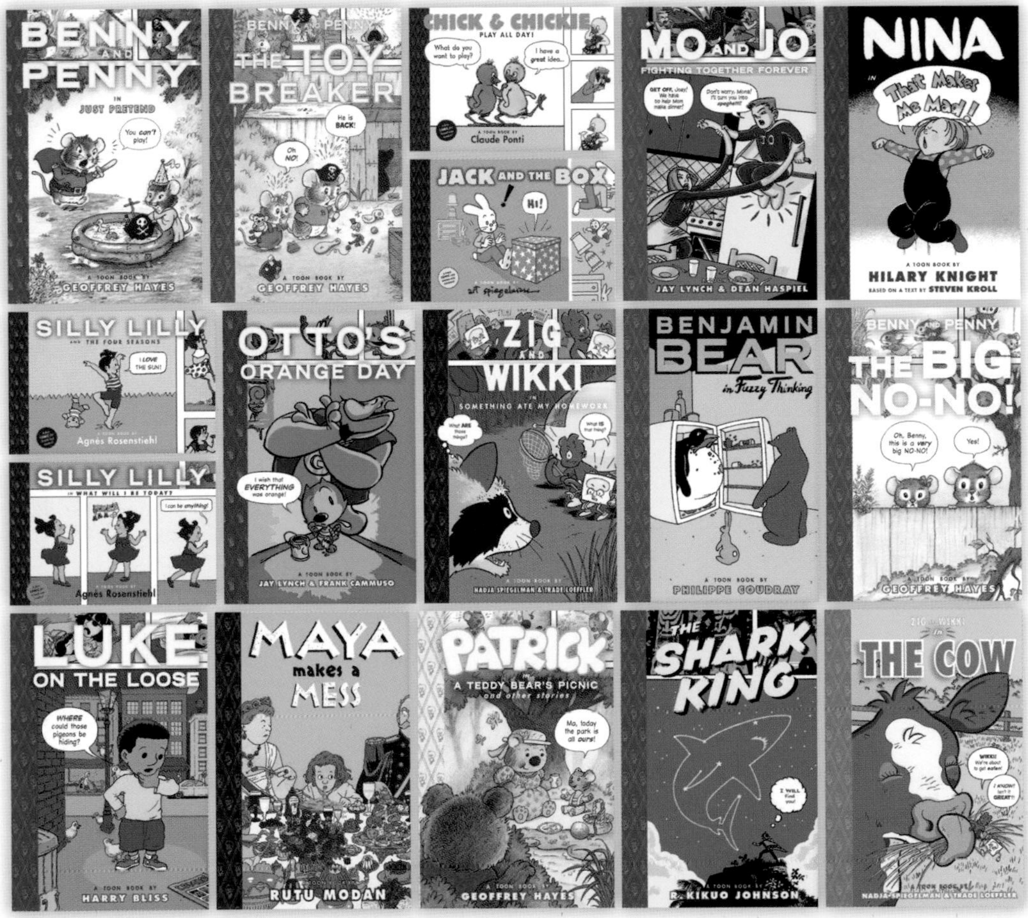

BENNY AND PENNY
IN JUST PRETEND
You can't play!
A TOON BOOK BY GEOFFREY HAYES
BENNY AND PENNY
THE TOY BREAKER
He is BACK!
Oh NO!
A TOON BOOK BY GEOFFREY HAYES
CHICK & CHICKIE
PLAY ALL DAY!
What do you want to play?
I have a great idea...
A TOON BOOK BY Claude Ponti
JACK AND THE BOX
HI!
A TOON BOOK BY art spiegelman
MO AND JO
FIGHTING TOGETHER FOREVER
JAY LYNCH & DEAN HASPIEL
NINA
IN
That Makes Me Mad!
A TOON BOOK BY
HILARY KNIGHT
BASED ON A TEXT BY STEVEN KROLL
SILLY LILLY
AND THE FOUR SEASONS
I LOVE THE SUN!
Agnès Rosenstiehl
SILLY LILLY
IN WHAT WILL I BE TODAY?
I can be anything!
Agnès Rosenstiehl
OTTO'S ORANGE DAY
I wish that EVERYTHING was orange!
A TOON BOOK BY
JAY LYNCH & FRANK CAMMUSO
ZIG AND WIKKI
IN
SOMETHING ATE MY HOMEWORK
A TOON BOOK BY
NADJA SPIEGELMAN & TRADE LOEFFLER
BENJAMIN BEAR
in Fuzzy Thinking
A TOON BOOK BY
PHILIPPE COUDRAY
BENNY AND PENNY
THE BIG NO-NO!
Oh, Benny, this is a very big NO-NO!
Yes!
A TOON BOOK BY
GEOFFREY HAYES
LUKE
ON THE LOOSE
WHERE could those pigeons be hiding?
A TOON BOOK BY
HARRY BLISS
MAYA
makes a
MESS
RUTU MODAN
PATRICK
IN
A TEDDY BEAR'S PICNIC
and other stories
Ma, today the park is all ours!
A TOON BOOK BY
GEOFFREY HAYES
THE SHARK KING
I WILL find you!
A TOON BOOK BY
R. KIKUO JOHNSON
ZIG AND WIKKI
IN
THE COW
A TOON BOOK BY
NADJA SPIEGELMAN & TRADE LOEFFLER

TOON BOOKS SET 1

Set of 10 hardcover books	**978-1-61479-298-7**
Benny and Penny in Just Pretend	978-1-61479-148-5
Benny and Penny in the Toy Breaker	978-1-61479-149-2
Chick & Chickie Play All Day!	978-1-61479-150-8
Jack and the Box	978-1-61479-151-5
Mo and Jo Fighting Together Forever	978-1-61479-152-2
Nina in That Makes Me Mad!	978-1-61479-153-9
Otto's Orange Day	978-1-61479-154-6
Silly Lilly and the Four Seasons	978-1-61479-155-3
Silly Lilly in What Will I Be Today?	978-1-61479-156-0
Zig and Wikki in Something Ate My Homework	978-1-61479-157-7

TOON BOOKS SET 2

Set of 8 hardcover books	**978-1-61479-298-7**
Benjamin Bear in Fuzzy Thinking	978-1-61479-299-4
Benny and Penny in the Big No-No!	978-1-61479-300-7
Little Mouse Gets Ready	978-1-61479-301-4
Luke on the Loose	978-1-61479-302-1
Maya Makes a Mess	978-1-61479-303-8
Patrick in a Teddy Bear's Picnic and Other Stories	978-1-61479-304-5
The Shark King	978-1-61479-305-2
Zig and Wikki in the Cow	978-1-61479-306-9